I0731887

Range Detective

by Warren Wendover

This initial novel is dedicated to Vikki Chenette, the wife of my friend, Tom Spence. She is a good and critical listener.

Published by:
Powder River Publishing LLC
1014 Black Mountain Road
Thermopolis, Wyoming 82443

Copyright © 2023
ISBN: 978-1-956881-36-3
Printed in the United States of America
Front cover design: Nora Villalobos

www.powderriverpublishing.com

Table of Contents

Decisions

I admit it. The decisions I've made in life so far haven't always been the best. They seemed okay at the time, or at least like they might be fun. That's how I started riding bulls. I remember my first bull, Slammin' Sammy, from the Snead Ranch near Pocatello. Later, I got better, but never got really good at it. Still, Mother Brindle said to me, "Gabe, just like your father said about you, 'He ain't pretty, but he's mine.' Same thing with the decisions you make. You can try to run away from them, like your worthless father did. But you gotta live with them." I didn't like to hear her talk about my dad that way. He was slow and easy; he never ran anywhere. That's how I remember him. He left on the day he dropped me off at the schoolhouse for my first go-round of education.

My mind's drifting back while I'm on Pete, my mare, in a shallow draw. Low clouds, moon behind them somewhere. Riding night herd ain't fun, but it's my decision, my job. Len Flegel's been losing cattle since he brought them off the forest permit earlier in the fall. "This land is your land, this land is my land…," Woody somebody sang. You can't beat a grandfathered lease.

Yesterday, Flegel and I toured the edge of the pasture in his pickup. I turned down the opportunity for a closer looksee when the ravens departed. There's not much to learn from an old gut pile. But he was being rustled, plain and simple—that's what he said. Now, just killing time, I clear the handle of my odd-number Smith and Wesson and dismount with my penlight to confirm what my nose is telling me; another kill, not very new. Satisfied, I lead Pete to a spot where I can remount. I just don't have that bounce anymore.

Rustling is part of God's great plan. A drought down around Texas and Oklahoma, and hay prices go up. Ranchers up here cut their herds and sell hay to their southern cousins. Good money. When the Texicans and the Sooners can't afford it any more they cut their own herds…, a second time. The price for beef on the hoof dips and bounces, but eventually, with fewer steers to market, beef prices go up like they have a plan to stay there for a little while. New ATVs replace horses. The animal rights folks—and they have their rights—resist the horses to dog food part of the cycle and arrange adoption ranches. Bottom line: You can't get $500 for a good cow pony but a fall steer at $1.60 a pound on the hoof, leaves the sale barn for $1,500; a cow/calf pair can fetch $1,600, or more.

This figuring kind of kept me awake in the dark in Len's pasture. Like the God crowd says: "He works in mysterious ways." Thinking about it, which is what I'm doing, cattle are pretty valuable property to leave out on a couple of thousand acres of fall pasture with nothing between them and the open road but four strands of rusty barbed wire propped up on rotted posts. "Put temptation in front of an honest man and he'll be dishonest soon," Mother Brindle used to say. And she wasn't sure how her sons were going to turn out. As they did, one is in the Colorado State Pen, and the other is a broken down ex-rodeo jock. I try not to pass judgement on kin so I wouldn't say which one is worse. And after my pop left, mom didn't have any use for men anyway. Still, she hoped she'd live long enough to spit in his eye should he ever come sneaking back for something of his she hadn't sold. He didn't and she didn't. Calculating life's odds does help pass the time, but I'm getting chilly.

I'd never carried any shiny on my saddle—no silver conchas, no metal covered stirrups; nothing on Pete's headstall either, and she rides with a sweet-iron bit. The grips on my S and W are black rubber. I'd rather not attract attention while I'm alone in the dark, unless I'm in my bed; and, heck, if old Finagler scares himself with a dog dream, and needs somebody to sleep with, he can find me by my smell.

Anyway, a steer's worth a lot and is pretty vulnerable out here. And a range detective—that's what I think I'll call myself tonight—trying to catch a rustler in the dark doesn't want to make himself conspicuous, for certain. A fellow who'll steal a steer is more dangerous than a fellow who'll steal your wife, I always say— well actually, I just thought of it while I'm out here getting chilly in my saddle. And, anyway, I'm not married, for which the women of the world must be silently grateful.

I go up to peek over the bank at the herd. They're scattered, but mostly bedded. There's a little bit of herd-noise, cows talking to late spring calves, steers bellyaching to one another, cud belching adding to the world's methane load, I'm told. But no lights, no sounds.

There's been frost since Sunday night. I pull the strings on my black sweatshirt hood. I don't wear a hat for night work. Not much sun to worry about, and nobody around to impress with my special crease. That is, unless I'm caught under a full moon. My dome's as shiny as fool's gold. I used to know a cowhand who slept in his hat, ever since someone in a bunkhouse prank took a shit in it. That was the story anyway. Damn, the things you think about when time's creeping. It's going to be a long time till morning. Pete and I might take a slow circle, not disturbing the herd, just a looksee.

I had pulled my two-horser around to the backside of Flegel's calving sheds a little after sundown, lights off, driving by twilight. I rode Pete into the pasture on an old hay-wagon rut on the opposite side of the pasture, away from the section line fence—pretty much a straight shot from the county road. Whoever was stealing steers unwired the chained gate at the section road, then tied it back up when they left. That wasn't a courtesy. Len and I figured they were hoping to return for a second dip. Cows wandering around out on the road would have attracted attention.

Earlier in the day, Flegel had called me. We found the tire tracks at the gate, but indistinct. What wasn't hardpan on the section road was dust. "I ain't even goin' to count head," he said. "Too many draws and yee-yaws to look into. The only accurate count I'll get is at the corral. But, I know guts left over after dead and gone, or can smell 'em, one."

We drove a little way into the pasture, across a couple of dips where a half-dozen ravens were scrabbling. "That there's your evidence," he said "Two ways to count. Just like in the war. We used to say 'add up your swinging dicks and your stinking corpses and you get your total.' That's your body count." I don't think he was trying to be amusing.

We returned to his barn. He pulled in beside his barely year-old John Deere and shut down.

"Pretty tractor," I said.

"You can buy one of them on a couple of methane wells if you toss in your takings from a half-dozen loads of hay sent down to the panhandle. But they don't make those Deeres like they used to," he said.

Pete's a good mare, Morgan and mustang. Stocky, not too far off the ground. I don't get around as good as I used to in those days when I thought I was something. No going back. My opinion of myself changed when a son of that dappled killer, Prince of Darkness, pile-drived me at Parsons Stadium down in Springdale, Arkansas. I didn't finish the season, and barely had enough money to get home after they turned me out of the hospital. I've been living with a bad hip nailed together, and a left shoulder that has a bit of flop to it, but not much strength, for the twenty-odd years since. Add a couple of dozen extra pounds and you got a pretty good picture of what a broken-down rodeo cowboy looks like. But Pete's "bucket trained," that's what they call it around here. She'll stand by an overturned pail while I use it as a step to get my foot in the stirrup. A bottom corral pole, a cut bank, a gullied cow path will work too.

Pete and I make our way around the pasture, using all the

dips and draws we can, keeping low. Cloudy still, quiet. When I've made most of the circle we go by a few ditch-watered cottonwoods where we jump a white-tail deer. After Pete's through dancing, I loosen my slicker from the saddle strings and put it on. It isn't likely to rain, but the slicker stops the breeze which is starting to kick up.

I spend the next couple of hours dozing, or trying to, or thinking about the things I'd rather be doing. Every half hour or so I ride up out of the draw, just high enough to look over the pasture, hoping to catch some lights up by the section road. Nothing.

Morning comes, but not too soon. It's grey. I'm stiff, my hip's paining. I turn Pete back toward the trailer. When I get there, I unsaddle and throw my tack in the back of my pickup, damp side up. I take an old gunny bag and rub Pete's wet back—more of a back scratch than anything, but that won't keep her from rolling when we get back. She'll come to her hay pile looking like a bad stucco job. No matter, she didn't come to much of a sweat except under the blanket. I drop the bit and let her hop in the trailer on her own. She always finds the way she likes to ride.

We drive past the calving sheds which are about a half mile from Flegel's house. Flegel told me that his wife, Sandra, when she was still around, didn't like the smell. She had him build the new sheds downwind from the house, and fence in a new holding pasture. Len used to tell her that the odor she was belly-aching about was the smell of money—or so he said.

You can't blame her for trying to get away with as much as she could when she left. But she was diddling Norton Weems, the John Deere salesman from Billings, who sold Len that tractor in the bargain, and she got caught—well not with her pants down, more like her skirt hiked up. The funniest thing, though, was that she never removed her glasses, even for pretend passion. I had it all on the DVD. That was my first job for Len Flegel, getting the pictures of his unfaithful wife and that would-be hotshot who sold the green giants. I made Len Flegel a happy man. Not that Flegel was ever so happy that you'd notice it. And too boot, Sandra could just as well have hired me to do a spy job on him. Len had been girl-friending with a senorita down in Casper for years, or so I heard. Word eventually gets around. He just had a sneaky nature about him, and his ex-to-be didn't find out about it until it was too late. Maybe the woman down in Casper, thought she was next in line to be Mrs. Leonard Flegel. Wrong. Len said there were about three things a person ought to try only once in life: being born, being married, and dying. His unnecessary conclusion was: "I only got one left on that list."

People said Flegel had a hole in his bucket, always complaining about what was leaking out. Ranching can do that to a fellow. "You may outlast it, but you ain't gonna out guess it," he said to me more than once. Well, didn't I know that? I'd done my turn at trying to ranch, after the son of Prince of Darkness ruined my rodeo career, but I wasn't the heir to any deeded land, and I got into ranching with low cash reserves. Still, I lasted just long enough for the '87 blizzard to wipe out most of my mortgaged herd. Next thing I know I'm hauling my fifth wheel double-axle rig—the only thing the bank left me—down to the Three Forks Trailer Park. Then I went and lined up with the other bozos who were peeing in Dixie cups in order to get a CDL so they could drive tankers and pipe-loaded flat-beds out in the gas fields. I did that for a few years and saved a little money. Then I started spending that rainy day fund until in a moment of sobriety I decided to take an on-line correspondence course to become a private detective. It was either that or getting licensed to sell real estate. But I got my principles, such as they are.

I found forty acres that was producing a fair crop of cactus and thistles, and had a dead cottonwood, wind-stripped of its bark The acreage was going for cheap. I moved my rig out onto it, got

Sorge Mallin to drill me a well, and while he had his backhoe out there making a drilling pad and a mud pit, I had him scrape out a septic pit and leach field. I put up corrals and a small pole barn, bought some hay, and a year or so later I buried Pete's predecessor, Moriarty, in the clay bank behind the dead cottonwood. Sorge excavated that hole for free, sensing family bereavement. How I came by Pete is another story.

I wasn't valedictorian of my mail correspondence detective class, but I got by. And I was offered the "Golden Graduate Program" whereby I could become a "master sleuth." That offer came with a couple of regional weekend seminars to which my performance qualified me. My family's motto "Jack of all trades," forbade aspirations of mastering anything, so I followed the correspondence trail to a license, a bonding agency, and a permit to carry concealed. And I took two weekend seminars which were freebies, always watchful for a sleuth-ette. But no Nick and Nora. Still, progress. In a few months I had gone from a dipsy-doodle out in the gas fields to a private detective. No clients to start with. But the correspondence school said my name was in their files and that I'd have referrals right away. I guess I was supposed to believe that. While I was waiting for my first job as a snoop, I went back to driving water tankers, on-call, piece work; I even helped Sorge Mallin drill some water wells. Still, I let it be known behind my hand that if an investigation was something a person was needing, then I was the local, affordable, if not the logical, choice.

Surprise, surprise when I got my first call. It was one of the lawyers in town who needed some subsurface water table analyses done very quietly so he could drop the hammer on a drilling company, WyoServe, for his client. What the hell did I know about water contamination—except what Sorge and I were guilty of? But, that's what we folks in this occupation do—get it done, or get out of the way. Long story short, I found a guy who worked for an environmental company up north and was willing to moonlight weekends using the company's equipment and lab connections. We did the cover-of-darkness thing on an offending well head, got the tests to the lawyer; he blindsided WyoServe. They wanted to settle quietly out of court because they had bids on a pile of federal leases which they didn't want to jeopardize. The lawyer and his client, Basin Environmentals, a nuisance group which had found its own racket, were so happy that I got kissed on the cheek by a leathery faced old hen in orthotic sandals, and a check that convinced me for the first time that I had made the right career choice. Hardly broke a sweat. Word gets around. There's been no looking back.

I'm about to get into my pickup when I see Norma Smith come from behind the Flegel ranch house headed my way in her white Ford with mud adornment all around. I close my door and lean my butt on the front fender. Norma pulls up.

"What's going on Brin?" she asks, window rolled down, she spits. Her seat's all the way forward and I know she's sitting on a cushion. She's built low to the ground, but she likes to ride around with her elbow out the window like one of the boys.

"Didn't you stop at Len's house?" I ask.

"He wasn't home," she says and wipes a dribble of Day's Work off her chin. "But my, you're up early."

"I couldn't sleep."

"Conscience bothering you? That happens to peeping-toms." She pauses for my reaction. "Going riding?"

"Might could."

"Looks like you've been," she says spotting my saddle blanket.

"Breaking in a saddle."

"You've had that saddle forever, I'd bet."

"Slow to break in," I say.

"Yep," she says.

"Everything fine at the sale barn?" I change the subject.

"Far as I can tell. If they got a scar or a notched ear, they're as good as branded in my book."

"Well, you would know."

She spits again. "See you," she says, turns her pickup around and leaves.

Norma comes from the long lines of the Smiths and the Craytons that go all the way back to the range wars. She had kin on both sides. Her family has probably smeared more brands with a running iron than there are ticks in a coyote's ear. But that's tradition for you. One century you're a killer or a bandit, but when they're looking back, you become a colorful fellow and you're due for a resurrection in the movies, and in the brochures done by the Chamber of Commerce. So, nobody really cares that a great, great granddaughter of paid assassins and lynch mob organizers intending to clear out the homesteaders ends up applying for the job of county brand inspector. She lives with her brothers out on lower Nine Mile. She's held the job for quite a while and has never impeded livestock commerce by making undue demands for authenticity.

Wednesday, sale days at the barn, she spends her time signing carbon copy affidavits certifying the transfer of stock from seller to buyer. If a brand isn't clear, or is missing, or is bright red and smells like it had been done in the trailer that morning, a nod and a wink and a ten-dollar bill will make the most ambiguous situation clear up. The pink carbon sheet makes it all official.

I check my hitch and brakes, then pull around past Len's house. She was right. His pickup is gone. I'll call him later.

Two Liars Make a Conspiracy

I come through town on the old highway, the one that was jilted by the interstate, but much of it's still in local use. I head on out to my cactus and thistle nature preserve, without stopping at Welles' Pit. Normally I would have had breakfast—crowd or no. This morning I'm too beat to eat. The old carcass doesn't take to all-nighters like it used to. Back then, when I was still rodeoing, after the show was done, I'd finish off the night shooting pool, or dangling long necks from two fingers of the hand I was casually pressing into the small of the back of the woman I was dancing with. Sometimes, I can almost remember how it felt to be young and on top of the world, or at least within sight of the top. I hope none of those rodeo ride-alongs remember me. I fancied myself a lover, but, well, my ears burn. Mother Brindle would say, "A fool fools himself first." I doubt any of them were fooled. There's a moral here: never believe anybody who groans back, "Oh baby!" Two liars make a conspiracy.

As I'm turning off the highway, the propane truck is idling by my gate. Jensen, the driver, rolls down his window. "Brindle," he says. "I'm on my way to Willyville. I stopped to see if you were getting low."

"I think I'm not due until next month," I say.

"Well, shit, I know that. How long have I been delivering propane?"

"Trying to dump stale gas on me?"

"Gas don't get stale, but I thought... ."

"You drew an elk license."

"How'd you guess."

"And if you could get a little ahead you'd probably be able... ."

"I need a week off." he smiles guiltily. "Season opens the twentieth."

"Which way's the price of gas headed?"

"What with demand, and all... ."

"I can't afford it, then. I'm on the pay-as-you-go life plan."

He nods understanding. Jensen revs the truck and pulls slowly onto the highway.

I turn Pete loose in the corral. She doesn't need any oats, but she's a good girl, so she gets a couple of handfuls of sweet grain anyway and a fair flake off a bale. I check her water and store my tack in what I call the barn. Ol' Finagler doesn't even come off the steps to say hello, but he thumps his tail on the planks as I pass him to go in. That old boy has some hurting going on too. He hasn't done any super-dog tricks for more than a couple of years. But he enjoys the sun when it's up high enough to reach the steps I built at the trailer's back door. I don't like to think about the day, maybe sooner than later, when I'll have to consider what's the humane thing to do. But, until then, the old boy has earned his peace and pleasure.

It's bedtime. But I always sleep sounder during the day with a medicinal double shot of Evan Williams. Works in the evening too. I'm living proof that there's nothing wrong with whiskey that a little moderation won't make worse. Following that rule, I do it again, make a stop at the couch, go to Turner Classic—nothing there I want to watch—so I give the clicker a kicker over to daytime TV. The ads add up, and the next thing I know I'm stumbling around looking for the bathroom and the sun has slipped down toward the hill behind the corral. "Well shit!" I say. Not that I've slept past an appointment, but I've dribbled in my shorts. I finish peeing in the shower while I scrub down, dry off, then choose some garments from my evening wardrobe—sweatshirt and Wranglers less soiled than the ones I left.

After that, I feel improved enough to go for some coffee. "What the hell!" I can't be drinking coffee this late in the day. I'll never get back to sleep. This is an example of how shift work can kill you, turns your whole day catty-wampus. I douse the burner

under the pot and go to the fridge for a beer. I need to get my bio-
logical clock back on schedule.

A second beer and the appetite starts to wake up under my
ribs—a good sign. I put some beans on to warm, and while I'm at
it toss out the shrunken lettuce from the bottom of the fridge. A
little grated cheddar, salsa and tabasco, and some soda crackers,
make the beans almost flavorful. A football game is on the TV. I am
trying to decide which team I don't want to win. I don't really care,
but Nebraska's a neighboring state. Still, it's got the longest, most
boring stretch of I-80 you could ever imagine. That's something
serious to hold against the Huskers. On the other hand, when I was
still riding bulls, I knew a rodeo clown from Missouri. He was a real
prick. So, I settle on lukewarm for Nebraska. My cell phone rings.

"That you, Brindle?" asks Len Flegel.

"Depends," I say.

"Were you out there all night?"

"Yep."

"What'd you see?"

"Cows, steers, a few late calves."

"No visitors?"

"Nope. Oh, and a deer."

"Hmm. Thought they'd be back."

"Me too." Huskers score. "Norma, stopped by as I was load-
ing up."

"What'd she want?"

"Guess she was looking for you. And she seemed to want to
know what I was doing up all night."

"How'd she know you were up all night?"

"She didn't, but she spotted Pete and my horse trailer."

"Pete who? I thought you were working solo."

"Pete, my mare."

"Oh. So, what'd you tell Norma?"

"Nothing." Mizzou kicks a field goal.

"That's one nosy gal."

"Well, she knows her brands. They all look the same to her after the slaughterhouse gets the hide off."

"Did she ask about me?"

"Nope."

"Did you go in the house?"

"Nope. I gotta have permission, or a reason, or an emergency. Didn't have any of those. And remember, just because I'm on your payroll, doesn't give me leave to poke around your palace."

"Thought you might have been looking for me."

"Your truck wasn't there."

"Fucking truck! You coming back out here tonight?"

"Didn't figure to. I thought you liked that truck."

"I liked what Sam Elliot said about one that looked like it on the TV, but he never had to change a blown radiator hose on it."

"That happened last night?"

"Down toward Larry the Trader's. You know, the old cowboy code, a man in need?"

"Yeah, I've fallen for that one a couple of times."

"Well, Nickel Lyder—remember him?"

"Runs a janitorial service."

"Yeah. He happened along in his van about an hour later and gave me a ride into Casper. It was after ten, so the auto parts store was closed. I called the emergency number. Some kid come down and found a replacement for my hose. I picked up a couple of hose clamps and bought me two of those five gallon gas cans and filled them up with water at the spigot. Since the kid lived in Bar Nunn he said he'd drive me back up and hold the flashlight while I replaced the hose. I tipped him, I hope it wasn't too much."

Flegel, usually a man of few words was telling me a whole lot more than I needed to know about his pickup's blown radiator hose. I figure he was creating a story about where he was when a cow thief got shot in his pasture.

"Somehow those boys—whoever they are—knew the herd is being watched," I said. "It was a perfect night for them, but they didn't show."

"Might have just been passing through. Picking and choosing," he says.

"Maybe." I have a thought. "You didn't mention this situation to the sheriff, did you?"

"Dickie McDo-nothing? That fat fuck."

"Careful how you talk about us fat fucks, Lenny."

"Want to know the difference between you and him?" Of course, Len doesn't wait for me to say I'm busting out with curiosity. "Main difference is that you ain't sheriff, and if you caught a rustler you probably wouldn't read him his rights before you shot him.... Would you?"

"That all depends," I say. "I think that's what law enforcement does—or supposed to."

"Who the hell cares. A dead rustler has already stopped listening—or rustling." He clears his throat at the other end. "Anyway, next move?"

"We'll wait."

"Wait for what?"

"That's why we're waiting, to find out."

"Maybe you should go back to takin' pictures. Catching rustlers may not be your thing."

My correspondence course only talked about an "exciting new career." It didn't say that my clients wouldn't be pains in the ass. But, under "Relations with Clients" it suggested: "Being 'on retainer' is the best way to take on what may be a continuing investigation." That was a formal way of saying, squeezing the teats on the cash cow.

"Don't worry, I got a couple of other angles working," which sounds good and it might buy me a little time to think of something.

"You watching the ball game on channel ten?" he asks.

"Nope. Never watch football. Who's playing?"

"Nebraska and Missouri."

"No kidding. Who you got?"

"Missouri," he says. "In Nam there was a guy from Nebraska in my company. Damn near got me killed. Never forgave Nebraska or his lame-brained parents for that."

"I know what you mean. But, I'd better go. Some of these hot leads are cooling."

A Night's Sleep

I get ready to go back to bed, but in a serious way this time, on the box springs. Though I recommend distilled spirits, my rotation on the night shift has my gut screwed up so I just settle for another beer. I turn on my little black and white TV at bedside. That's the other dish mounted on the barn roof. I watch Brazilians, Texans, and North Dakotans—all foreigners—ride bulls. One did eight seconds and then a snow angel dismount. The bullfighters did a great job distracting the bull, and the rider gets up and walks away like, "it ain't nothin'," brushing the arena dirt off his butt. I can imagine him back behind the chutes puking and then popping something of the pain-killer variety, after the obligatory Alie Dee interview, and the Tuff Hedeman commentary. Sleep kind of eases up on me like ol' Finagler when he wants up on the bed. Like I say, super-dog's way in the past—no bounding. The subtlety of old age. You hardly ever know when he makes his move, but when you wake up... , there he is.

In my case, I get woke by a knock at my door which won't go away. I notice the TV channel is into its vacuum cleaners and sex toys early morning segment. Finagler has roused himself to growl unenthusiastically. I keep a semi-antique H & R .44 hanging on a peg, next to where I hang my coat. I take it down.

I've always thought a good way to get assassinated, if that's the plan, is to stand behind a door made out of thin aluminum sheet and two inches of injected foam, and ask, "Who is it?" So, I'm off to the side when I ask, "Who is it?"

"Sheriff McDougall."

"I'm putting this gun away, Sheriff." I say loudly, then swing the door open. "Come in," He does.

"Pardon the mess," I gesture behind me. "But they deported my Mexican maid."

The floor creaks under McDougall's weight. "Why don't you get your pants on."

"We going somewhere?"

"Not yet. But I don't like to look at your knobby legs."

"Can't blame you," I say. "And I don't like folks looking at them either. I'll be right back." From around the corner I shout, "Have a seat, Dick, but do 'er easy. You've put on a few pounds since your last campaign picture." Tit for tat.

I come back, sucking up my belly, buttoning my jeans. "So, what brings you out to shady acres at this time of the morning?" I ask.

"Why were you out at Flegel's last night?"

"Who says?"

"Norma."

"Well, that woman.... Just because I was parked behind Flegel's sheds, and she was over by Flegel's house a little after sun-up, and she probably saw me closing the gate as I left his pasture.... That don't prove I was there."

"You were in his pasture?"

"One of them. "

"Which one?"

"Ask Norma."

"I'm asking you."

I'm not about to give up my cattle rustling investigation to this office variety Matt Dillon. That's one of the meanings of "private" in the occupation of "private investigator." And he isn't paying me. "Like I told Norma, I couldn't sleep."

"Couldn't sleep. So, you drove out in the dark to take a ride in Flegel's pasture?"

"They didn't waste that sheriff schooling on you, Dick."

"And you were out in his pasture all night?"

"What'd Norma tell you? She doesn't lie. But is that enough of a reason to come out here at one in the morning? A fellow can't take a ride with his best gal? What's the world coming to?"

"Who's your best gal?"

"Pete, my mare, for crying out loud, Dick." I wait. "So, are you going to tell me what this is all about, or just arrest me for riding my horse in the dark?"

"That's what I'm trying to figure out."

I wait.

"Remember Sandra Flegel?" he asks narrowing his eyes.

"Vaguely." Another evasion. I picture momentarily some of my favorites clips from the DVD I turned over to Len.

"When was the last time you saw her?"

I think back, not counting a couple of days ago when I played my copy of the DVD rather than renting a pay per view. "I passed her in the hall in the courthouse when Lenny and she were making their break-up official."

"And since then?"

"You said the last time, that was the last time; about two years ago."

He reached in his jacket pocket, pulled out a pair of broken spectacles. "Want to tell me about these?"

"I had the laser surgery when I was still driving water trucks and I could pay for it. They aren't mine."

"Well, I know that. But I found them in your pickup, under the seat."

"You were in my pickup?"

"In a manner of speaking."

"You got a warrant, or at least a probable cause?"

"Probably."

"You didn't find those in my truck, whoever's they are."

"Sandra Flegel's" he said. He pointed to an embossing on the inside of one temple. I couldn't see it. "She took back her maiden name. It's Johnson."

I reach; he withdraws the glasses. "Don't handle the evidence," he says.

"Well, you are."

"I'm trained." He puts them back in his jacket pocket.

"I don't much give a fuck, Dick! But you didn't find them in my pickup."

McDougall shrugged. I shrugged back and waited.

McDougall didn't do drama very well, but, after the dramatic pause, "Len found her face down in his kitchen. Not much left of the back of her skull."

Even real surprise looks suspicious to a suspicious cop. And if you don't act surprised that's suspicious too. I tried to split the difference, chewed on my lip, shook my head slowly from side to side, sad eyes. "Dead?"

"Don't get much deader."

Got any suspects?" I asked.

"I'm talking to him," he says. "You're the one who took all those pictures on that DVD?"

"What DVD?"

"The one we found by her body. Except for that tractor salesman's little dick and pimply ass, those could've gone direct to the Hustler channel."

"How do you know that Romeo is a tractor salesman?"

"I'm asking the questions."

"Okay, ask me why I want to know."

I clamp down on another comment bubbling up. Instead, I say, "I've heard they teach investigating skills in sheriff's school…." I stop there before I suggest that Norma might have done it, or Flegel. It was his kitchen. But trying to divert attention is another thing that raises suspicion. I give him the "next?" look.

He looks back, and then he tells me to put on my shoes and we'll take a ride down to his office.

Lawyering Up

Ever since I got into this profession, which isn't very long, I've thought that I should have a lawyer—I hardly know one. But I've never followed up. I don't count the lawyer that handled Flegel's divorce or the ambulance chaser who on behalf of his client sued the gas field driller. I didn't pay them, they weren't in my service. But when I leave McDougall's office, I think, maybe now's the time.

In this town, though, lawyers sue each other's clients just to stay in practice, and then play pick-up basketball together at lunchtime in the old high school gym, and swap stories in the shower. If you're a lawyer in Fort Fletcher, code of ethics doesn't count, and you may have to represent both sides in order to make your office rent. Your best shot at a living is defending rich kids' DUIs and small-time meth and pot busts off the bench, subbing for the public defender, and installing lawn sprinkler systems in your spare time. Gillette's a better place to look for a lawyer.

I'm so wired about what McDougall is trying to pin on me that I can't get back to sleep, so I fire up the coffee pot again. I take another shower and get ready to drive to the center of the world's carbon footprint.

The night before, while the graveyard shift jailer and 911 operator, Louise, filed her nails, McDougall pretended to call the judge. Apparently, the pretend judge said to turn me loose until McDougall got some more evidence. So, while he's working on that, I'll go on over and hire me some counsel. I call ahead.

I pull into the lot in front of a two-story building with phony weathered plank siding and a sign intended to resemble something out of a sound stage western. Décor in the waiting room is more of the same. A buffalo head in a prominent spot, a pair of antelope, mounted to look alert instead of dead. A painting that's a copy of someone's copy of that Charlie Russell waterhole fight. Chairs made out of elk antlers with seats made of coiled lariats. The receptionist wears an Annie Oakley skirt and robin egg colored cowboy boots.

"You're Gabriel Brindle," she concludes after I tell her.

"You can call me Gabe," I say. "All my friends do."

"I'm not your friend," she says without looking at me.

"Yet," I correct her with a smile.

"Please wait," she says. "Mister Woo will be with you shortly."

"Mr. Woo?" I ask.

"Yes, John Woo. A lawyer who recently joined the firm."

Jesus Christ, I say to myself. Sheriff's trying to frame me up for murder and I get me an Asian lawyer. I was thinking someone along the lines of a Perry Mason. I sit down and thumb through a Western Horseman magazine. I don't get past the Wranglers ad, tight on Miss Rodeo USA's ass, before a lean Japanese man steps into the waiting room. "Mr. Brindle?" he asks.

I toss the magazine on the coffee table and stand up. "That's me," I say and take his waiting hand for a quick shake. He's casual, in a western shirt and bolo tie, dress code for line dancing at the Stomp and Shout.

"I'm John Woo. This way," he says and departs down a long hall, skylights and high-hung ivy baskets. A nice effect.

"Is that real ivy?" I ask as I follow him, as if I gave a shit.

"No. Watering it on a ladder... if someone fell... or fell on someone else..., a law suit...." He doesn't finish his sentence, interrupts it with a titter, and leads ahead, then stands aside while I enter his office and he pulls the door closed behind us.

Inside, small, no windows, recessed fluorescents, a desk and lamp, flat screen and keyboard; loaded bookshelves behind him. "It's not fancy," he says. "But it's home."

"The good-looking lady in the baby blue boots said you were new," I say.

His look is dismissive. "Titles and ranks. I tried private practice for a while, actually did some work for this firm, and against it. They decided to give me a 'join 'em, don't fight 'em' offer. So, I'm here. Today's newby is tomorrow's junior partner."

"Well, you Japanese are known to be ambitious, or so I hear."

"Chinese," he says.

"Same thing, right?" Ignoramus that I am, I forge on.

He doesn't say anything. He just focuses past my shoulder and waits.

I look around. "Well, anyway. You got the law books to prove you're a lawyer, that's for sure." I gesture the shelves behind him.

"Embossed wallpaper," he says. "All the statutes are on DVDs, or you can get them off a website."

"Yeah, that's what I meant," I say. Why don't I just shut up?

He takes a deep breath. "You think you need a lawyer. Why?"

I tell him about McDougall, the glasses; then back up and tell him about Flegel's divorce and the John Deere salesman and the DVD; then I back up again and tell him about the rustling in Flegel's pasture and Norma the brand inspector.

"It's bullshit," he says.

"What's bullshit?"

"The 'looky, looky what I've found' tactic. I call it, 'the grab your nuts in the elevator' tactic, just to see if you'll say 'ouch.' Your sheriff didn't find those glasses in your truck. They might not have even been hers, or he picked them up off this guy's kitchen floor."

"Kinda like a case we read in detective school." I sound so much like a simpleton, I blush.

"State of Florida v. Dr. Neptune," he says. "The Ski-doo jockey kills the dolphin trainer. A love triangle."

"Yeah. That one." I say without a clue. "You studied it too?"

"That case was thirty years before DNA. But that's the trouble with these satellite industries around law enforcement. They're so cheap they only borrow stuff whose copyright has run. Where'd you say you studied your craft again?"

I like the sound of that, my craft. "Drummond Detective," I say, squaring my shoulders, sitting up a little straighter.

"I thought they closed up their post office box and went out of business."

"Wasn't my fault. I paid good money…."

He waved his hand as if to say, 'neither here nor there.' "I wouldn't worry about your situation. All they got is a body at the mortuary—the guy that files the report is the mortician who's grateful for the business. Small towns almost always get the two for one. Your sheriff will have had a deputy take some pictures, and dust the place for fingerprints—send the whole kit to the FBI. They'll do the DNA profiles, polymerase, if they're not too busy. If they come to you for a swab or a cuticle, that's when you should call me. But your sheriff's dumb enough to place a bet in a frog jumping contest at a Cajun cookout."

I had never heard that one before. Kinda cute, my Chinese lawyer trying to talk local—well, local if this were Louisiana. I was starting to like this guy. He seemed a regular sort, didn't sound foreign at all, and had a sense of humor. "Sorry about the slip up on the ethnic thing," I hear myself saying, while I'm saying to myself, shut the fuck up!

"Nothing," he says and stands.

"Well, yeah," I say. "My point was…"

He saves me. "If you want to retain our firm, leave a check with the receptionist." He hands me his card and holds the door as I leave.

I stop at Annie Oakley's desk to find out how much John Woo is going to cost me on a try-out basis.

"So?" she raises her precise eyebrows.

"I think I'd like to hire Mr. Woo," I say.

"Billable hours or…?"

"Your best bargain," I say.

"Five hundred dollars will get you started," she says.

It ain't classy to swallow twice and roll your eyes. I learned that riding bulls. If you have walked through the door, or into the arena, don't let them see you sweat, as the saying goes. I can ride this ton of bull that wants to kill me, no problem, or in the present case…. "That's all? Heck, a half-day's work." I say.

She looks at me with an excellent version of boredom and disbelief.

I could have asked her to bill me, and then beat it; but, I actually think I'd like to have Woo in my corner if it comes to that. I pull out my checkbook and write a check, hand it to her. I might have to go back to driving a water truck in the gas fields to cover it.

She prints out a receipt and hands it to me. "Have a nice day." Why would she lie?

"Likewise," I say. "It's been a pleasure." Why would I lie?

Petunia, Flower of the West

When I get back to Fort Fletcher, I pick up a few trailer house supplies—they usually come in cans and bottles—and go on home. I notice biodiversity springing up in my nature preserve—fall-sprouting cheat grass by the mailbox. Finagler is glad to see me, but he doesn't get up until I go to the sack of kibble. Then I go back out to feed Pete who is also glad to see me. A flake or two off a bale gets her attention focused. I fill her water trough.

I used to know a rancher down on Blue Creek. He wasn't fond of quarter horses since one left him walking down off the mountain in a snowstorm, with a navicular bone all gone to hell. "I let him carry my saddle down," he said. The poor gelding had to be shot. His owner claimed that breeding had weakened the quarter horse bone structure and mass. "Leave it to humans to screw up a good idea," he said. He claimed that mustang blood in any horse would improve it in all ways: physically, intelligence, attitude.

How I came by Petunia: She had caved in a farrier's ribs. She was headed for a one-way to a Canadian dog food cannery. Just a coincidence that, I'd dropped by her owner's place to jaw a little. We had been on the bull circuit together years before.

He wasn't a horse man in any true sense—as far as working things out with one who was getting the signals wrong. He was a bull rider, and gimped-up one too, as most of us ex-bullriders are to one degree or another. Still, he liked to keep a couple of horses around to help him remember how things used to be. Like a lot of us, he got a little misty looking back. He'd had a Morgan mare who got some fence breeding by a mustang stallion over around White Mountain. That was shortly before he relocated up to these parts, and we reconnected driving water trucks to the drillers.

That winter he farmed out the Morgan—down to southern Colorado where his cousin lived. Driving truck in the snow—chaining up and the rest of the mess— was bad enough. But when drilling slowed down he hired out for night calving during the season.

That set off his old injuries. He rode an ATV in the calving pasture and bought enough hay for the holdover horse. He didn't need another horse to take care of. But the next spring when he picked up the mare she was plump as a pumpkin. He named the foal Petunia, tamed her down, did a little ground work on a lunge line, some work with her feet, and a little trimming, but it killed him in the back to do much of it. Still, she'd never kicked him, he said, if you don't count the hair-trigger reflexes which foals can't help. She was kind of a pet. At a long two he took her down to Kaycee to let Buck Ordingham put thirty days on her in the wet blanket school of horse training.

Buck said even though she was a little short and a little chubby, she was as good a horse as a fellow would want. Of course, Buck always complimented the horses he rode out. It was good business. But at the time, my friend believed Buck was straight honest about Petunia.

Then came the farrier. The first kick Pete gave him put him down. And except that my friend jerked her off balance with the halter rope she would have struck the farrier a couple of times more as he was trying to get up. He might have ended up as a damp spot in the corral.

When he got his breath back, the farrier judged her to be a born killer. He was ready to go at her head with a set of nippers, but my friend pushed him away. Still, that was enough to set my friend against her since he was about ready to give up the pretense of riding anyway—too many pains. He was just getting by, and willing to shed the cost of hay and horse doctoring. He called the horse trader who had already sold the Morgan for him, and told him to come pick up her three year old daughter, and take her to the "sale barn." It was common knowledge that surplus horses got one trip through the sale ring. If a horse didn't inspire enough of a bid, it was no-sale and a one-way trip to Canada.

Glad I got there at the right time. My friend had already made the deal, money had changed hands. It cost me a hundred more to get her back off the trailer. I had seen her before, and I just liked the look in her eye. It wasn't a killer look, maybe a little prideful, but pretty wise for a long three-year-old.

Later I found out I'd made the right move. That farrier had a temper and was in the wrong trade for a horse beater. Pete had smelled it on him and got in the first shot. It's amazing what a little understanding will do for a smart animal. And most of the dumb critters are walking around on their hind legs and wouldn't know a friendly gesture if it licked them in the face.

After feeding Pete I go back to the bunkhouse and twist off a top, just to keep in practice. I sit down at the table to call Flegel. When he answers, he seems a little skittish. But I know why I called him, so I just jump right over that. "Len, it seems to me you got more to worry about than a few steers walking off without their skins in the night."

"Hell, I do," he says. "That's all I'm worrying about."

That stops me for a second. "Well, Len, not to be insensitive and stuff, but what about your ex ending up dead on your kitchen floor?"

"Dickie McDo-nuthin' said not to talk about that."

"Well, shit, Len. He tried to wrap it up the next morning in the middle of the night by layin' it on me. What the fuck?"

"Don't blame me. I didn't send him anywhere."

"I didn't say you did."

"Any fool could see she wasn't killed in my kitchen. She was all bled out before whoever did it drug her in and left her on my floor. There was a little blood smear on my steps, but that was it."

"Be goddamned," I say. "Trying to frame you, you think?"

"That's even dumber than your first question."

I didn't remember asking a first question, except, 'what the fuck?' "What then?"

"Beats me. But life goes on, and I got dollars on the hoof in that pasture. You coming back, or do I have to turn this investigation over to Dickie and spend my methane money on Conchita?"

"You seeing her again? I thought you were avoiding commitments."

"Well, she's not all that bad. She still has a little go to her."

"If you have an urge to talk to McDougall, don't let me stand in your way. I'm paid in advance to the end of the week, and we'll part ways. No regrets. If you can get Dicky out of his office chair, then....and we're still friends."

He ignores me. "That's where I was heading when the hose blew on the goddamn Dodge."

"To see McDougall?"

"You're not as smart as you think you are."

"That's not the nicest thing you ever said to me, but close."

"I was on my way to Casper... to see Conchita."

"It's all clearing up now."

"Gotta hand it to her. She worked her way up in that homemade, home grown style supermarket, and then got to be regional rep when it was bought by those brothers up in Seattle—or Portland—I don't remember."

"Does it matter?"

"Not hardly, except I like to know what I'm talking about."

"Good luck on that."

"And they bought another store. She's on a first name basis with this warehouse in Billings."

"She's having conversations with a warehouse?"

"Damn it, Gabriel—you know what I mean. And those kinds of grocery stores are going to put us ranchers out of business. Plus, putting a woman in charge don't help none."

"You're a bellyacher, Len," I say. "But deep down...."

"And shouldn't I be? Bad pickups. Women takin' over holding out until they get what they want."

"Well, Len, my Dear Abby on that is…."

"I ain't paying you for that. All I want is to get my herd secure. I'd go out there myself tonight if I wasn't going to a goddamned birthday party down in Casper with that woman."

"Sounds to me like Conchita's got you by the co-johnnies."

"Like I said, I ain't paying you for advice."

"Well, I was never good about personal relationships anyway—but if you'd kick in a little more methane on my fees…. And not to get personal, but that Dodge—I say keep fixing it until it's paid off, or Sam Elliot shuts up—whichever comes first. That's what you call your maintenance. Of course, as soon as it's paid off the engine'll blow. And as far as your cows go, let's wait a few days. I say let's settle for letting things settle. Loose lips—well, I can't remember how that goes, but they used to say it during the Second World War. I saw in in the movies."

"What the hell are you talkin' about? You weren't even born…."

"Still, like I said, let's wait a few days. Okay?" I can't help it, so I ask. "You taking her a birthday present? I'd suggest something shiny…."

"It ain't her birthday. She just wants us to show up at someone else's party."

The Prettiest Horse

I've never been comfortable with the idea of shooting a person—you know, intending to kill him. After all, why else would you shoot a person. Not saying I wouldn't do it—like if I had to in order to save my own hide... that sort of thing. But, just pulling down and shooting someone, like in a firing squad, or as a hit man. I think a fellow ought to be personally motivated if he's going to kill someone. Not to say that everyone doesn't have the right to be dead, at least once. But I don't want to be involved if I can help it. Like they say: the most satisfying work is when you can put your heart into it.

Vietnam was over by the time I was old enough to do some serious thinking about shooting someone, or alternatively, crossing the border to Canada. Eventually I did—cross the border— to the Calgary Stampede. And the military is all volunteer now. Leonard is a generation before me. He's a Vietnam vet. When I asked about his service, he changed the subject. Stupid question. I got the message. Probably no one who was in country during the war came out untouched if they came out at all.

That's life for you. Much of the time it's just the luck of the draw. Like blackjack, or bingo—or bull riding, or in Leonard's case, the military draft lottery. But some chancy games will get you killed, and you don't know that trouble is coming until it's already there.

Being prepared to pull the trigger is one thing, while pulling it, I imagine, is a whole other matter. Still, shooting someone in self-defense— I don't mean like that asshole down in Florida. His version of self-defense was theoretical. Theoretically anyone is a threat—a human being, after all—even more so if he doesn't look like you. Shoot first, ask questions later. Slow down there, buckaroo. I like a little more mystery in my mysteries. What about your motivation, for instance? Those steps are in the wrong order. No, I mean if someone's coming at you. Your first question's already been answered. My odd-number S & W should lay him down, but I'd hope he wouldn't die. That's when I'd be looking to "hand off my case-work" to the authorities as they explained it at Drummond. Yep, in short order. In fact, that might have been the way I visualized it might happen—if it ever happened, which I hoped it wouldn't. Then, I could cash my check, and go back to watching old black and white movies in the company of Evan Williams.

The bull on the final go-round up in Calgary gave me a good ride and earned me some money. His name was Trigger Happy, one of the many sons of Hair Trigger, who is in the Hall of Fame. See how life becomes poetry if you wait long enough? And true to form, most of us are still waiting.

I make a guess that Flegel and I aren't the only ones who know he's headed back to Casper for the night. Well, Conchita, for one; who's she talking to? And even though I told Leonard I wasn't riding his herd that night, a little white lie can help along an investigation. As I say, I turned down the Master Sleuth post-graduate registration, but I'm current on my studies in front of the TV.

I park my horse trailer behind Len's house, in front of his pole barn this time. It's an extra half-mile ride into the gate than if I had parked behind his calving sheds as I did before, but, someone might have seen me over there two days ago, you know, glassing from the hill behind the county road or someplace else, wherever. This is about the best I can do for stealth.

I saddled Pete before I trailered her from my Bonanza spread, so all I have to do is to give a tug on the latigo, use the running board to mount, and we are on our way. The sun has been gone for a half hour. Pete remembers the wagon road. The moon isn't due until after eleven, so I'll be well in place by then. Thank goodness Len isn't totally a Mr. Tidy. I use an old post pile to mount after I close the gate.

I circle. I don't want to disturb the herd which should be

mostly bedded. Pete and I find the ditch cottonwoods and settle into the routine of every half hour riding up for a peek-see. I've dressed a little better, an extra sweatshirt, got the strings pulled and tied under my hoody. I am dozing in the saddle, having run out of matters for speculation. Pete jerks her head around, and I'm on the alert. Even before I get up to the rise, I can see parking lights of a vehicle sweeping the rim of a draw about a quarter mile away. No hurry. Just like when you're angling for catfish—let 'em enjoy the bait and get focused on their job, then set the hook. Well, I don't fish, but I've seen a movie called "The Southerner." I think that's the one where a catfish is hooked. If it can happen in the movies on my TV, then it can happen anywhere.

I take my field glasses which are hanging on the saddle horn and try to get a look, but it's amazing how bad binoculars are in a situation like this. If I do much more of this shift work I'm gonna have to spend some money with Cabela's and buy some low light peekers. I'm carrying a Navy Seals type balaclava so I untie my hood and slip it on—might have done that before. But it itches. Now I want my face covered. Then Pete and I start circumnavigating—I believe that's the word. I first heard it in a movie about Captain Cook on Turner Classic. In other words, I plan on using their trailer the way a basketball player goes past a pick to the backboard. My God, TV is instructive.

I can see from where I am that one of them is out with a flashlight. A few cows jump and bolt, but one steer stops to look back, dazzled by the beam. A chirp-hiss of a silenced gun and the steer goes down. The partner of the guy on foot must have been in the pickup, because the rig starts rolling slow, just parking lights, and a flashlight out of the driver's window. Once he's got the steer lined up he goes dark and rolls toward the kill and the one on foot steps off toward another pair of steers. Shortly another muffled shot, another steer down not far from the first. He bends over the head of the second, comes back to the first; he must be bleeding them.

I figure like the other times they're planning on leaving with only hanging carcasses--guts and hide in the field. Better to leave the brand behind. But I figure wrong. They're in a hurry. The driver goes by the downed steers, backs around, then gets out. The open door flashes a pale dome light. I get a glimpse of a short stocky guy in a cap, sweatshirt hood up. Probably has the same hat rule that I do. No sunbeams, no brim. Door closes, light's out. He uses a flashlight to see, goes to the back and swings the trailer door open. He must have a winch bolted at the front of the trailer. He backs out pulling the cable off the spool.

It's funny how experience can fill in what's going on by the way a person is moving, but now I'm close enough in a little coulee to start to see what I've been describing to myself. The guy who's done the killing hands the gun to the other fellow who drops it through the window into the cab of the truck. Tall guy opens up a hock on the first steer. His partner hooks the tendon and using his corded pushbutton starts reeling in the catch, lifts the rear hooves clear, and all the way in.

They move to the next, the one closer to me. I wait till they they're guiding it over the back of the trailer, then goose Pete out of our hidey-spot, drop the reins on her neck calf-roping style, and shout "Good evening!" I punch their pupils with my three cell. Three-five-seven is in my other hand.

God, that's a good feeling, when a plan comes together! But it doesn't last long. Still, for that moment you could have convinced me I was an honest to god range-riding Pinkerton in control of the situation—just like in the movies.

The two of them are startled all to hell. "Keep your hands where I can see them," I say, straight out of the scripting department. Pete is prancing a little. This is more excitement than she's had since she kicked that farrier. To boot, she's smelling the blood that's pumped out of the two dead steers.

The tall rustler looks into my beam, so for a moment he's not sure if I came with an army. He takes a step toward me. The other one in the cap, dives under the gooseneck of his trailer. He's out of my sight. So much for the element of surprise. It can slip right through your fingers like a twenty dollar bill at the bar.

The tall guy reaches past the steer which is half in the trailer. He spins and comes at me with what looks like a gun. Well, that was a moment when shooting first seemed to be the right option. I let fly. Dropped him just clean as you please while Pete, startled, spins and humps. I hit the ground.

I've landed hard getting off a bull, had the wind knocked out of me, been briefly unconscious, but that was when I was trying to plan a dismount, had a rodeo clown between me and the bull most of the time, and EMTs behind the chutes. But looking back, this dismount must have had all the elements of spontaneity to it, and with the extra weight—if I remember my Isaac Newton—added to the overall effect. I'm not sure how I might have looked to them, but by the time I come to my senses, they're gone. My balaclava's twisted to cover my eyes, my face is resting on a clump of rabbit brush.

It's easing over toward dawn when I sit up, pull off my headgear, look around. Pete's nowhere to be seen. I pat myself down like a guy who's been sleeping one off in a bus station, just to see if he still has his wallet. In my case I'm looking for jutting bones. I seem intact, but I taste blood in my mouth, and feel a flap of my cheek hanging inside. I stand up. I'm not steady, but at least every limb is moving. That's when I spot Pete's head raising up the next draw over.

I can tell by the look in her eye that she thinks she's done something wrong. But she's not apologizing. That was a loud noise! In horse language she's saying, funny he's never dismounted that way before... and I helped.

I look around where the rustlers' trailer had been. No body. And the drag marks in the grass and brush tell me the driver took off with the steer only half in the trailer and the door flapping. By God, I'm hurting. Enough CSI. I need to get out of here.

I ease my way over toward Pete. She backs away snorting. I talk to her, extend my hand, but then back away a couple of steps. She steps forward. I wait. Then she lets me take the cheek strap; the reins have slipped forward but are still looped behind her ears. I reassure her we're still friends, slip the reins over her head and lead her back towards where my gun might be, unless they took it. It's halfway down in a tangle of sagebrush, but I spot it. I flip open the cylinder, blow the dirt out of the barrel and holster it.

I lead Pete over to a wash, put her in the bottom, and from the high side I'm able to get on board. The ride back is painful to say the least, but walking back would have been worse. Like my friend down on Blue Creek used to say, "the prettiest horse is the one which takes you back to the corral."

Where Doesn't it Hurt?

Len Flegel must have been watching me leave his pasture. By the time I get to my pickup he's standing by my trailer, and Snickers, his heeler is beside him. He has that look on his face that asks, "What?"

I have my own question. I thought he was going to be in Casper. "How was the party?" I ease myself down off of Pete with a groan.

"Them parties ain't near as much fun as you might think," he says. "But damn, you're a little creaky."

"That ain't the half of it," I say. "Did you hear my shot?"

"You been shooting? I just got home about an hour ago."

"Just once."

"When?"

"Maybe sometime after one."

"That'd be when I was sleeping on Conchita's couch. Made her mad again. When I got up to piss, I just said, 'Fuck it!' I'll go home."

"I guess I only winged him," I say. "Or his partner threw his body in the horse trailer with the steers they shot."

He helps me unsaddle Pete and tosses my gear in the back of the pickup while I tell him the whole story. Pete steps into the trailer and he swings the door closed. Snickers nips at my pants.

"If your heeler bites me.... "

"She don't bite that hard." He gives her a kick. "Snickers!" She yips and sulks away. He points silently to his pickup and she jumps up on the lowered tailgate. "So, you think you got one of them." He smiles. "By God, that's the kind of report I've been waiting to hear. I'd bet my lucky rabbit's foot they ain't coming back."

"Well," I say. "Finding a replacement for an honest partner in crime, one you can trust can't be that easy."

He lifts the tailgate to his pickup and slams it shut. "Stay!" he commands Snickers. He starts towards the back door of his house. "Come on in. I got some coffee, and I can rustle up a little horse liniment for your bumps."

"I think I'll just haul the works back home."

"You're not going to talk to McDougall, are you?"

"Rules say you're supposed to report a shooting. Of course, I can't prove anyone's been shot with no body laying around."

"If you turn it over to Dicky he won't solve a goddamn thing—like catching both of them, for instance—and your hands'll be tied."

I know what he's saying is probably true. I'm told that Mc-Dougall has more cold cases than a Budweiser truck, but once you're on his screen, just to appear busy, he'll come back to harass you if it doesn't take too much effort. "Well, gunshot wounds end up in hospitals, or dumped in the ditch." I could have added, or on your kitchen floor.

"Anyway, that about wraps 'er up, for now, I guess, huh?" Flegel says. "Hope he's cold and stiff by now."

"I have no idea where I hit him," I say. "But life isn't fair. He might survive." From me that's not irony, but I don't think Len knows. I open the door to my truck. "Better go." I get in like an old man, back the trailer around, and leave. My hip is paining like a sonofabitch. I drive home, put Pete in the corral, feed her, check her water and un-hitch. I can hardly crank down the strut. Finagler eyeballs me from the step.

I'm going out the gate to the emergency room at the Health Center, Jensen, the propane guy flags me down from the shoulder of the road. I pull around, half on the highway. "What?"

"Can I top it off for you."

"I told you, I'm not due till next month."

"I know, but...."

"Sorry, gotta go," I say while tonguing the cut on the inside of my mouth and trying to find a comfortable spot for my ass.

I pull into the patron's lot at the Center. I'm stiffening up bigtime. As I walk toward the emergency entrance, somebody I should know is coming out, arm strapped to his side. "How you doing, Brin," he asks through the gritted teeth of pain.

"Fine," I pause my limping gait. "And you?"

"Fine," he says and continues toward his car.

Stupid. If we were "fine" we'd be someplace else.

I report to the desk. By golly, there's Frankie. She doesn't seem glad to see me, but she's the intake person in the ER, all professional-like. And it's not an old friends' get together.

"How can I help you?" she asks.

"Had a little horse accident," I say.

She slips a clipboard with a form and pen across the counter. I look at her and I shake my head. "I'm hurtin'," I say.

"Just sign. You can read it later."

I sign.

"Have a seat. We'll get right to you."

"Is it alright if I stand and lean?" I do, and shortly, they do. Nurse takes my vitals. Dr. Rangle's on duty. I've known him since I came to Fort Fletcher. He always looks as if the weight of the world were on his shoulders.

"What happened, Gabriel?"

"Got off my horse kinda funny."

"Where'd you land?"

"In the pasture." I say.

He sighs. "What part of your body did you land on?"

"I'm not sure. When I came to, I was face down in a clump of brush."

"Bleeding anywhere?"

"I bit a chunk out of the inside of my mouth."

"Don't bull riders wear mouthpieces."

"C'mon, Doc."

"Okay, where does it hurt?"

"Where doesn't it."

He hands me a gown. "Put this on." He turns to his laptop on the counter and makes a few entries. Everything has gone electronic now. Saving paper, saving clerical worker wages, waiting for the next solar flare or hacker to wipe out the whole fucking system.

"Hop up here," he says and pats the bench with the clean sheet on it.

"You're kidding, of course," I say as I ease up.

He doesn't smile. "Lie back." He lifts my legs at the calves and extends the support. He palpates—that's what they call it. Sounds more professional than squeezing and poking. I wince a couple of times. "I'll give you a little something for the pain, but I'd better get some pictures first. Can you walk?"

I am not overcome by modesty but the idea of people I don't know looking at the crack of my ass in a gown that's open all the way down the back, while I gimp my way down the corridor and across the hall to the x-ray room, just doesn't tickle me. "Can I ride?"

"You mean a gurney?" A sly smile.

I nod. He leaves. Shortly a CNA—I gather because her name tag says: "Dana Procter, CNA"—arrives and gives me a hand up. It strikes me funny that since she's in a uniform with a title, I don't mind that she sees me this way, gown slipping askew, scar on my right hip from the surgery, cowboy tan, white above the hatline... and thin on top. As she wheels me, I consider asking her what CNA stands for, but the pain helps me grit my teeth and shut up.

Doctor's Orders

The x-ray jockey helps me lie down on his cold table and takes quite a few pictures. While I groan and turn on my side, he moves the crosshairs to a different part. Sheriff McDougall steps in the room, then leaves. I guess he wasn't looking for me. Then Dudley Morton, the game warden, steps in. Same thing.

I hear the two of them outside the other x-ray room. "He says he shot himself in the leg while he was hunting," says Morton.

And I say to myself, put a gun in the hands of a dipshit and he'll probably do some damage, alright. Then I realize in a flash that I'm a bonehead, and they may be talking about my rustler.

Dicky McDo-nothing says, "They're taking him to surgery. Did he show you his license and I. D?"

"He says he lost his wallet up on the mountain."

"Did he drive himself down?"

"His hunting partner dropped him off in the middle of the night."

"Well, he ain't going anywhere. We can question him some more after they clean him out and sew him up."

"Helluva time to be hunting, probably spotlighting. Better be able to show a license or we'll write him up multiple for a court appearance," says Morton. "Right now, he's a self-confessed hunter from South Dakota without a license, who shot himself in the leg."

"If you want to believe that," says McDougall. "Could have saved himself a lot a trouble if he just said his wife shot him. If he don't want to press charges against her, and somebody'll pay the bill, case closed!"

I wouldn't be Sam Spade of the sagebrush if I didn't finally prick up my ears. I actually don't get all of it, but I am able to fill in what's missing. The x-ray guy finishes up with me, I get settled on the gurney again. He summons a CNA and I get a ride back to the examination room.

Doc Rangle scrolls the x-rays down on his laptop. He says "hmm," and "hmm."

I wait.

"Nothing's broken," he says. "And the screws in your hip held."

I absorb the good news.

"So, just strains, sprains, and pains," he says, a practiced diagnosis that doesn't do justice to how I'm hurting. "Tylenol or Advil," he concludes the interview. "Whatever you're used to taking that doesn't upset your stomach."

"I'd opt for some oxy-whatever," I say.

"You're the only one who knows how bad it hurts." He points to the childish scale of faces, from a frown with tears on one end changing to a smile on the other. "Where do you place yourself on that hurt scale?"

"I'm with that Pac-man who's crying." I point to the face on the far right of the scale—overstated, but I want some pills.

"He's laughing." Rangle's playing with me, the sadistic fuck. I guess I push his buttons.

"Well, that's where I'm at."

"Opioids, strong stuff," he says. "And not cheap. You have a prescription plan?"

"Sure do. Pay as you go. Give me a double. What I don't use I'll sell out behind the Exxon station." At the thought of some pain-killers I'm already feeling better.

"Have it your way," he says and scrawls something on a pad, tears a sheet off, hands it to me, and leaves.

All I'll have to do is drive down the street to the drug store, flash my credit card, and sign a form with my address, to get some happy pills.

At the intake/discharge desk Frankie nods. "Want a copy of what you signed?"

"Sure," I say. I lean on the counter, beckon Frankie to lean my way. "The hunting accident …."

She narrows her eyes the way she used to when she was telling me to back off, and I wasn't even getting close yet.

"Who was it?"

"Out of town," she says.

"Where'd he shoot himself?"

"You ever heard of doctor/patient confidentiality?" she asks. "Same goes in the emergency room."

"You didn't feel that way in the old days when you were preg-testing cows at the vet's shop."

"I'm doing healthcare now you may have noticed."

"That doesn't mean we're not friends, does it?" I wink. But the hurts are talking to me.

"You're pitiful." She hit a few keys on the ever-present laptop. I leaned forward to hear while she read: "Bullet wound, entering upper right adductor minimus muscle, striking right femur, diverting, laterally and downward, exciting lower lateral biceps femoris muscle."

"'What the fuck does that mean?'"

"Well, I think it means he'd have had to have a rubber arm and a double jointed wrist to shoot himself in the leg that way." She smiles at me, and I realize I'm having a good day after all. "Or he dropped his gun and fell on it."

"A couple of inches to the left and he'd have bled out before he got here."

"Thanks," I say. "I owe you one."

"You don't owe me a thing," says Frankie.

I wave Doc Rangel's prescription. "Gotta go follow doc's orders." I limp out. With pain pills it's kind of like whiskey—half the fun is in the anticipation. But that only lasts a little while.

Smoked Red Herring

Back at the mansion, I knock down a couple of oxys with water, no Evan Williams—I'm not suicidal, yet. Then, because this ain't my first rodeo, as the cliché goes, I top off my evening with a couple of stool softeners I picked up at the pharmacy. Hurting and feeling no pain at the same time, I sleep like a baby.

About nine that night I'm trying to get the kinks out before inventing and then starting my physical therapy. No stain, no pain, as we used to share behind the bull chutes. I start slow by doing some can calisthenics—Campbell's soup and a beer. I'm almost in a recuperative mood when Flegel calls.

"You weren't answering earlier," he says.

"Well, Jesus, Len, you got me working odd hours, so I was asleep."

"I want to talk to you."

"Talk away."

"You know phones aren't secure."

"Who says."

"I heard it on the radio."

"You think the government's listening to you? What do you know that they want to know?"

"It was on the TV, I think."

"What?"

"About the fucking NSA, or whatever. Sometimes you just have to take matters into your own hands."

That line used to get some leering laughs when I was in my high school locker room.

"Meet me," he said.

"Sounds like a dating service. Where?"

"Muddy Bridge."

Muddy Bridge crosses Muddy Creek which is hardly ever muddy. But whoever named it must have come upon the creek after a cloudburst. Even during the high water in the spring, the mountain snow melt is pretty clear, but a cloud burst can scour lower hills into the draws and gullies, and produce a brown soup and cloudy up the water for a half-day. Probably where the name came from. The Native folks must have had it named already, but no one consulted them.

There's no mystery why Fort Fletcher was built on the creek, about the time of Red Cloud's War. It was part of the string of forts along the Bozeman Trail. Now, tourists stop to see dioramas in the county museum and a few pieces of charred wood from the incinerated fort.

I park my pickup in the alley as if I were going into the back door of the Hide-Away Bar, then gimp-walk around to the bridge. I'm improving already. I lean on the rail and look down into the water, pill dreaming, studying the reflections of the streetlights which are posted on the walkway. I don't notice Flegel until he puts his hand on my shoulder.

I jump. "Goddamn!"

"You're a little frisky," he says.

"You startled me."

He studies the creek. "You know, about Sandra.…"

"She's dead, last I heard," I say.

"Well, what I meant is, about her…"

"I'd know Norton Weems's bare ass anywhere."

"Not that. Sandra wanted the ranch."

"I believe that's why I got involved, isn't it?" He's wasting time.

"All past history."

Isn't all history past? I'm thinking. "Well, I guess she's got over that urge. And you're pretty much clear of that, aren't you?"

We back away from the rail to let a fellow from the Hide-Away steady himself as he passes.

"She never gave up."

"You're not telling me anything. It was all on the DVD I gave you."

"No, I don't mean that way."

"But, like you say, past history. The curious thing is why she ended up dead on your kitchen floor—not that you hired me to think about that, so I don't. Anyway, you're alibied as far as I can see."

"Better than alibied," he says. "Unless you think I'd kill that woman and then drag her into my own kitchen. And besides after I changed that hose on my fuckin' Dodge, I went on to Casper, which is where I was heading in the first place. I don't need to explain."

He's doing a lot of explaining for a person who doesn't need to explain. Someone has a sick sense of humor to leave Flegel's dead ex-wife's body in his kitchen. But, I'll leave all the heavy thinking to the sheriff. I'm just a self-appointed mud hole Marlowe, and I'll stick with the cattle rustling.

"I was at Conchita's," Flegel says. His face tells me he didn't have a good time.

These women in Len's life just don't seem to go away—well, Sandra Johnson has gone. I figure she's still on a slab in the cooler of the mortuary awaiting directions from the next of kin—if anyone owns up. But Conchita? Habit, I guess.

"I think I know who killed her."

"Conchita's dead?"

"Sandra! Brin, you're a pain in the ass!"

"No shit?"

"I got no proof. And telling Dick McDougall anything is like pissing up a rope."

We look into the reflecting creek again, like a couple of lovers leaning our elbows on the railing. "Well, are you going to tell me, or not?" I finally ask.

"I thought you knew," he says.

"Like, I'm supposed to put two and two together, huh? Like

that, huh? Well, I'm not your Mr. Tibbs. Now there was an investigator!"

"Who?"

"Never mind."

"Tibbs, you say?"

"Yeah. We should all hold ourselves to the standards of our mentors."

"Yeah. Like a detective. This Tibbs fellow. Did you meet him while you were studying your investigator-type courses on that weekend down in Laramie?"

"I guess I told you about that, huh?"

"Yep. You were trying to impress me."

"In a way."

"So, have you talked to this Tibbs fellow?"

"It's too early," I deflect.

"Make a guess."

"Well, my guess would be the John Deere salesman."

"You'd better go back to driving a water wagon," he says. "Something you know how to do."

I'm ready to say, "Fuck you, Flegel!" But practical matters get in the way, so I say, "I could make a better guess if you gave me a little in advance, so I would have something to say thank you for around Thanksgiving."

I lean toward his shoulder and say, "The rustler ain't gonna die, but it was dark, and Pete was edgy. Anyway, I'm sorry I didn't need to get the sheriff out there to look at a corpse." Of course, I'm not really sorry. I have the rustler thing in a corner and I'm proud of that. The sheriff will slap the cuffs on him as soon as I step forward to explain. The so-called hunter will get scheduled for a trial. My reputation will get a boost a notch up from being a peeping-tom. And the bonus is that I didn't have to kill anybody, though I might have given it a thought when I saw that gun in his hand. "Progress is my middle name."

"Now, what the hell are you talking about?"

"Got us a wounded rustler recovering in the hospital."

"You're full of shit. Who wounded him?"

"Your night-riding Nick Charles." I try to suppress a note of pride as I point to myself with my thumb.

"You were out there while I was down in Casper? You told me you weren't going to ride?"

"I changed my mind."

"What's his name?"

"Not part of my job. Dicky McDoo and the Game Warden..."

"What's the Game Warden got to do with it?"

"Rambo the rustler says he shot himself in a hunting accident."

"But you did it?"

"That's what I'm trying to explain. Which ought to garner me a little advance on the week's expenses..."

He looks at me. I make like I'm ready to leave.

"I've been meaning—" He reaches into his shirt pocket and pulls out some folded bills, holds them above the railing. I put my hand over the wad. I still don't say, "Fuck you, Flegel!" I just think it. I'll count the money later. I slip it into my pants pocket.

He elbows me. "You won't tell?"

"It's hard to tell, But I'd guess it'll be in the newspaper on Friday."

"You're a cute one, you know that? You won't tell, so I'll tell you," he says with resignation. "Conchita did it."

I turn to look him in the eye, so I'm sure I get the joke. He doesn't crack a smile. "You're saying Conchita shot the rustler?"

"Oh for God's sake, Brin! I was at Conchita's. How could she shoot the rustler you just told me you shot? I was talking about my ex-wife."

"It's all clearing up now, Len. But I'm done with your ex-wife. The folks in the deep detective department where I enrolled say it's good to know when to move on."

"You know how you can smell something fishy?" Now he's playing detective.

I want to say that I'm smelling a load of red herring at that very moment, but I nod and say, "Well, that's a puzzler, Len."

"Yep."

I expect him to get around to a motive. I wait. He doesn't. So, I ask.

He shrugs with, "Who can figure a woman?"

"Not possible," I say. "But that's because women are smarter than we are."

"Don't I know it? I've never been able to."

"No. I mean, it's not possible this Conchita killed her. She's not that dumb... if she's a woman."

"Well, I don't mean she did it herself. More like a conspiracy."

"Are you okay, Len? I guess you've been having trouble sleeping. Watchin' too much TV."

"Wouldn't you?"

"Nothing that a little whiskey wouldn't tamp down. What conspiracy?"

"What I'm saying is she had it done."

"Conchita had it done? Like a favor to you? How do you gather that?"

"When I was down there, and she was in her bathroom..."

"Nature called."

"I looked on her phone. I copied down the numbers of her recent calls."

"Let me guess. One of them was your ex's."

"You got it."

"How do you know?"

"I dialed it, got her voice mail."

"On your phone?"

"On Conchita's phone."

"Proves what?"

"Proves they were conspiring."

"Did you listen to her messages or anything?"

"How would I do that, I don't know the PINs."

"Nothing, then, is what you can prove, and you say you were with Conchita when your ex got dumped in your kitchen?"

"Where there's smoke there's fire."

"I thought we were sniffing up fish."

"What fish?"

"Never mind."

"Sometimes you don't make any sense at all," he says. "But it's the same thing. When nothing makes sense, I get edgy. But I'll make it worth your time, you know. Bad enough I'm losing cattle, but now I'm looking over my shoulder. Snickers ain't a watch dog, just a damn good heeler. So, I can't count on her to watch my back. As I say, I'll make it worth your time."

"Len, I'm just a range detective, trying to catch some rustlers. With my help, the sheriff and the game warden have one on an I. V. drip in the hospital. So, I'm just about ready to ride off into the sunset (I drop to a dramatic baritone) on the 'case of the missing steers'—like in the movies. I don't do bodyguard work. Bull riding taught me that. Plus, I don't like you enough to be around you that much."

"Brin, I'm serious."

Imminent danger can put the whine in a man's voice, but it wasn't my turn to whine. "Just for a while," said Flegel.

The stool softeners interrupt our conversation. "I'll think on it, Len." I hurry to my pickup, stay puckered as I hurry home.

Corn Fed

Flegel hasn't shorted me on my fee, though we've never come to an agreement of what it is. He is an honest man in his way, but when I was a kid, Mother Brindle lectured us more than once about the dangers of being robbed by honest men. The reference to my missing father was pretty clear. And, of course, it was my brother, Isaiah, who because of an honest mistake was stationed at the pen in Canyon City. Still, Flegel hasn't double-dealt me, yet, though he requires a nudge now and then.

In a couple of days I'm feeling good enough to take a trip to Casper. I wonder what this Conchita is like, and why Flegel thinks she's involved in Sandra Johnson's death, not that it's any of my business. I remind myself that I'm just working on a rustling situation. Still, I'm on Flegel's payroll, so knowing a little more won't hurt me. A girlfriend involved in the killing of an ex-wife after the divorce would be a new one on me. But many things are, and anything's possible. That keeps my curiosity up.

One of the stock handlers back in my rodeo days used to amuse himself by getting into bar-fights, and occasionally winning one. "Make sure the guy you pick out for a fight doesn't have any friends in the place. Those are the ones that'll hit you in the back of the head with a table leg when you're not looking. Get to know what you're dealing with, then go for the gusto." His best advice, though, was, "Always pick on someone bigger than you. If you win the fight, you're tough; if you lose, you got an excuse."

I've been told there's only one store in Casper where you can buy grass-fed beef, free-range hen eggs, no BGH milk, and enough varieties of chemical fertilizer-free produce to fill your roughage quota and make you sick and tired of healthy stuff. The parking lot is well stocked with Land Rovers, Out Backs, and Priuses. The other vehicles-- some Sierras, Hummers, crewcabs— look as if they are embarrassed to be seen in that crowd. They should have a separate parking lot in a covered garage and a side entrance.

I go in. There are stacks of crates of fall apples on sale by the door, five pound tins of raw honey in artful pyramids, organically grown pumpkins (with a sign encouraging would-be druids, and others, to Party Like a Pagan! This must be the place, I say to myself.

I find the meat counter in the back, a long refrigerated glassed array displaying all sorts of animal protein: fowl, rabbit, lamb, mutton, pork, and beef. As far as the beef goes, and except for an example of each featured cut under wrap, all the rest is in large pieces behind a glass cooler door in various stages of being custom carved by the bunch of butchers with blood smeared aprons and gloves with the stainless steel wire woven through them. I get it. They only cut the meat, or grind it, when you order it. You can actually choose the percentage of fat you want in your burger. They have tubs of cubed beef, pasture veal, of various marblings. I watch as lean and fat, dark and tasty, lighter and bland, are fed into the maw of a grinder, reground and placed on a tray, weighed, and a price label for a customer. Fascinating!

I figure on ordering something so hanging around ogling the slabs of beef won't get me arrested as a pervert. I touch the little bell on the counter to which Juan—nametag, ID—responds.

"What can I cut for you?" he asks.

"What you got in the way of steaks?" I ask back.

Juan moves down the counter, slides open a pair of doors on his side of the case, leans in and starts touching cuts—all labeled—then back out to announce: "We got your sirloin, your New York strip, your T-bone, your rib-eye, your flank, your chop… ."

"Stop right there and back up." I say. "Let's try the T-bone," And then just to make sure he knows that I'm part of the movement, I ask, "Grass fed?"

"Yes, but if it's too lean for you, we have corn fed…"

"Feed lot?" I ask, trying not to overplay my mock surprise.

"Farmer's corral; organic corn, no antibiotics, nothing Monsanto. A happy steer."

"Well sure, organic corn fed is what I meant, what I want." For a moment I wonder how the emotional state of a steer preparing to die is determined.

"Which side of the steer?"

"Whichever one you want."

"I'll bring a rack from the cooler," he says and turns toward the large doors beyond the cutting blocks. "Be right back."

Juan returns with a bone-in loin hugged to his apron. He shows me the butt for my approval.

"Beautiful," I say, which is no lie.

"How thick?" he asks.

"Inch, or a little better."

"How many?" he asks.

"Two." Thinking about giving Frankie a shout. Maybe she's forgotten why she stopped answering my calls. And if not, I'll eat them both.

Juan turns back to a cutting block, slices the meat to the bone with a knife, then expertly cuts the bone with two whacks of a cleaver. I've never seen that—it's always a bandsaw which is followed with a damp rag of questionable cleanliness wiping off the pulverized bone and tissue. He places my steaks in a paper tray and wraps them in film. He punches in code, weighs them; the machine extrudes a price tag label, and he slaps it on my wrapped steaks.

The counter's not that busy, so when he hands me the steaks I ask, "Is this wrapping ...uh, environmental, Juan?"

He looks at me with the disdain I deserve. "Biodegradable," he says, and starts to turn away.

"All kidding aside," I say. "Is Conchita back there somewhere?"

"Who?"

"Conchita, the manager," I clarify.

"Why?"

"I'm an old friend," I say. An alias would be of no use. "I'm Gabe Brindle."

He sizes me up.

"I'll see if she's back from lunch." He goes to a wall pad, hits an intercom button, speaks, listens; speaks again, listens again. "She'll be right out."

While I'm waiting I find one of my business cards: *Need to Know? Complete and Discrete. G. Brindle."* Phone, e-mail. Something Drummond Detective helped me create.

I don't know what I expected, but Conchita, despite the look of annoyance on her face, is attractive and built like a proud fireplug with additions.

"What's up?" she asks.

"Gabe Brindle," I say.

"You Health Department honchos need to bother someone else. If we were any cleaner we'd be prepping for surgery." I like her spunk, her accent, the disdain of a Latina who speaks ESL like a weapon.

"I'm not the Health Department," I say. I hand her my card over the top of the counter.

She takes it, looks at it. "So?"

"Can we talk?"

"Why?"

"If we talk, you'll know why. Clear up the confusion."

"Who's confused?"

Juan idles behind her, scrapes the butcher block, wipes off the cleaver.

"Well, I am, for one," I say.

Conchita expels a quiet groan. "Come on back." She gestures to the set of swinging doors beyond the end of the counter.

As usual I've come to the point where my script fails me. I'm behind the doors with my package of steaks, following Conchita around cutting blocks staffed by a half-dozen butchers who are out-fitted with many sharp tools. Is this a good idea? Len's paranoia may be contagious.

The route circumvents the walk-in cooler. I peek through the glass. Enough beef to open a supermarket. Then I remember I'm in a supermarket. She gestures for me to follow. I do—down a hall, up a set of diamond-plate stairs to a landing faced by a wall which extends almost to the angling struts of the warehouse ceiling.

I apologize for my slow ascent. "My mare and I parted com-pany without warning," I say. She's indifferent. She swipes a card, the door clicks. Inside is a large boxy space, brightly illuminated by a skylight, and insulated from the hub-bub of the store and the sound of the compressors and evaporators of the meat coolers. A contemplative spot, an oasis from the protein mart below.

I look around, point to a door in the outside wall. "Where does the door go?" I ask.

"Outside stairs. Is this why you came by?"

"Not really."

"Okay. What's on your mind?"

"May I sit?"

She sweeps the room with her hand, a pair of over-stuffed, a couch, a treadmill. "Suit yourself."

The chair works for me.

"Like I asked," she starts again and takes a seat behind a butcher-block desk. "What's on your mind?"

There's a refrigerator under the counter on the back wall be-hind her. "Could you put my steaks in your fridge?" I extend them.

"You're not going to be here that long. So again, what's on your mind?" Well-spoken and the meaning is clear.

"It's who is on my mind," I say, settling my steaks on the

carpet by my feet.

"Have it your way. Who's on your mind?"

"Leonard Flegel. Len to his friends."

No reaction from her. Finally, "Are you asking me if I know Lenny?"

"Not really."

"What then?"

"Well, you know, his ex-wife's body got dumped on his floor. This made Len edgy, and left a mess on the floor." I lied.
"He don't work a mop too well."

"What's that got to do with me?"

"Did you know her?"

"Didn't know her. Knew of her. Lenny probably told you. He and I spent some time down here before they were divorced."

"But you like Lenny."

"I got to like him. But he complains a lot. He used to complain to me about her."

"Complaints are Lenny's stock and trade."

She shrugs a 'so what?'

"What'd he complain about?"

I can see she's processing. What to tell, what not to tell, why? And why should she, to start with? I learned in Drummond's correspondence school that it's not so much the answer as it is the pause after you ask the question that is the telling thing, if you can interpret the signs.

"Well, you know Lenny," she says. "And besides, he can't dance."

"He's kind of hard to get to know. When we get better acquainted maybe he'll ask me to dance."

"You work for him, don't you?"

I hadn't owned up to that. "I'm just trying to help. As they say, a friend in need, is a...."

"What, then?" she bristles.

"Like I say, if you're Lenny, and you get an ex-wife, back of the brain pot missing, cooling, dumped on your kitchen floor. It can ruin the rest of your day and half a jar of Mr. Clean."

"¡La puta!" she hissed.

"That's unnecessary," I say. "A little respect for the dead."

The veneer is off. She narrows her eyes. "She did Lenny some bad... some real bad."

I nod encouragement.

"Not that I should give a shit. The pendejo!"

"Now, now," I mock. "Lenny has spoken well of you."

"Lenny makes promises he don't keep."

"Well, you know, promises are forever, but circumstances change."

We're working up momentum. Pent up stuff can start, and you should stand back and let it flow. Another Drummond gem.

"I think he was sorry," I encourage.

"He tried to make me believe it when he came back."

"Ah, well, you know Lenny."

"But I don't believe it. He's too suspicious, and what he wants from me...."

"What?"

"Do I have to lie to get a favor now and then?"

"What kind of favor? What kind of lie?"

"What kind of pickup do you drive?"

"A G.M.C."

"Are they good ones—those Jimmies?"

"Runs."

"Well, I need a new pickup. I've always had a Ford—an old Ford."

"I should mention, Dodge Rams can blow radiator hoses."

"So I've heard."

"Anyway, I can't afford a new truck. And me and the bank don't talk when they say 6%. Not to mention insurance."

I'm wondering, why are we talking about pickups.

"Lenny could help me out," she says.

"Well, you know Lenny," I say.

Then out of nowhere. The leak that Drummond taught about. Handled properly, encouragement, understanding, acting like a priest, or a bartender. "It's amazing," said one of the cops at the seminar. "You can't get that sort of stuff with a good rubber hose." That hadn't crossed my mind.

"Lenny don't have no sense of his manhood. He thinks everyone is after his cojones. His wife, even after he divorced her, he thinks she was still figurin' how she's gonna clean him out. Probably deserved it. He done some pretty mean shit to her and she was fired up!"

I should know, but I ask. "What kind of shit?"

"Traded a good time with his wife for a deal on a tractor from that salesman up in Billings. Got a beautiful 7R. But a pickup? Sorry, Conchita."

"7R?"

"Don't ask me. I don't know tractors from nothin'. That's what he said when he showed me pictures."

"He told you he pimped his wife?"

"She didn't know it. She thought she was making her own deals, to mess with Lenny's head. You know, letting him hear some of her talk. Leaving her phone around so he could look at who she'd been dialing. Trips to Sheridan, to Billings. Like I say, messin' with his head. But his head don't need that. He does it to himself, better."

"Well, you know Lenny."

"Then he got some slime mirón to take videos."

I gather she is referring to me with that Spanish word. "Mee-roan?" I ask.

"Peeping Tom." She makes opera glasses with her fingers,

peers through them at me.

I shudder, shake my head in disgust. "That's pretty low."

"Then after she moves up to Billings, the bitch wants to talk to me!"

"I thought you said you didn't know her."

She looks at me with a load of superiority. "I read a novel. This guy is a hitman. His day job is an insurance adjustor. He has a family, he goes to soccer games, the PTA. His wife don't know him that well. She gets the cancer. He has, how do you say it? A moral dilemma—it's on the back book cover. Question is should he tell her before she dies that he kills people to pay for the treatments to keep her alive. He decides not to. That's as far as I've read."

I know the novel. And I've finished it. She dies. And he discovers some interesting things about his late wife. "So did she figure it out about him?"

"Who?"

"The woman in the novel, for shit sake?"

"I guess not. But knowing somebody means a lot of different things."

"Are you suffering from a moral dilemma?" I ask.

"Are you out of your mind?" She stands up, goes to the door of her space, opens it, beckons, steps aside for me to pass. "Ask one of the employees for a cold-pack, so your steaks don't get warm on your way home." To my back as I descend the stairs, "It's been a pleasure talking with you, Gabriel. Feel free to stop back anytime."

Just like that. Veneer back in place.

Friendship

I have time to think on the way home. I might hook up the old bunkhouse buggy and move someplace else. But then I think, there are fucked-up people everywhere, and I'm not in a self-imposed witness protection program... yet. I'm a has-been arena cowboy who's driven a water truck out to drilling rigs and put in a few years trying to ranch. I have no pension, and I'm a little over a decade away from Social Security and Medicare. Need to Know? Complete and Discrete starts to look better to me again. I cheer up which happens when your options are limited to almost none, the happy man headed to the gallows. Well, a little overstated but what's hype for anyway—driving home, mind wandering?

I pull off to the rest stop in Kaycee. One of the benefits of the interstate system. Beats the old style of squatting in the barrow pit after kicking the grass for rattlesnakes. Before I leave, I dial up Frankie's number, or what it used to be anyhow. It's her voice: "This isn't me. This is a recording. Leave a message."

"I got two righteous T-bones," I say brightly. "Your place or mine?"

I'd dated Frankie a few times. If you could call it that. We'd exchanged niceties when she was working at the vet hospital. Finagler liked her. She gave him his shots. Then she upgraded to the Medical Center. Let me put it this way: we parted friends, never got past that. She didn't like my habits or my sense of humor. Or the fact I wanted to stay over. Who could blame her? There's not a lot about myself I like that much either, no matter how I make the excuses. But you live with what you got.

A couple of years ago when Pete was cycling I left her in a fellow's breeding pasture with his good looking Paso Fino stallion—well, I guess that stallion was good looking, because he was the first and last Paso Fino I ever saw. He wasn't too big, had a good rump, and had Spanish horse pedigree, so I thought he might produce a good foal for Pete. That's the advantage of having a mare.

If you get a special one, you can try again. And, as much as I liked old Moriarty, they nipped his nuts when he was two. I bought him from a rodeo stock wrangler when he was twelve.   T h e n Morry did the inevitable—got older and died. There's a moral to this recollection somewhere but I'm avoiding it.

Pete might make a good mom, but I still have to find out because that Paso Fino didn't get the job done. I found that out when I took her to the vet. Frankie was assisting, and more. She was learning. The vet gave directions to her and she performed her first sonogram, Pete the subject of her attention.

Frankie couldn't find anything with the probe pressed against the colon wall, so the vet got impatient, had her pull out and tried on his own. But no implantation. Pete wasn't in a very good mood after that, but I invited Frankie for a beer when she got off work, just to show there were no hard feelings from either Pete or me.

The owner of the Paso Fino stallion wanted his stud fee. But I told him that I wasn't going to pay him for the privilege of having my mare kick his lover boy in the ribs. So, we split the difference: I paid, while he offered another forty-five days in the pasture, the next time Pete cycled. But Pete and I never went back.

It might have been on our third date when I had Frankie over to my place after a meal and a few beers at Howdy's Inn. I meant to, but I hadn't cleaned up the trailer. She looked around when she came in. She didn't say a word as I threw my dirty jeans on the bed so she could have a chair.

"I've been busy," I said as an explanation. "Care to get acquainted with Evan Williams?" I've always thought that it's easier to overlook a person's faults after a couple of good belts of whiskey; and my self-conscious lack of tact with women might be less noticeable if we were fairly sloshed. That was the plan I was working on. It had worked sometimes on the bull circuit.

But Frankie wanted to talk. She had her own needs. One of

them was to be treated as if she were special. Not too much to ask, but a person shouldn't ask. Still, she did. "What do you like about me?"

"You're a pretty good lookin' gal, for one," I said. That wasn't exactly true. But she wasn't bad looking either. She had intense eyes. Overall, she was well muscled, but not overdone, tight ass; a little flat chested, but I'm not nearly the tits man I used to be before silicone. I don't like body art or body sculpting of any kind. I used to try to work out with the weights at the local Y, but my God, they're heavy!

Just to play the game as I poured a little more whiskey over cubes, I asked, "What do you like about me?"

She scratched her chin. "Not much," she said, looking around. "Still you're better than most. And you offered to buy dinner."

"That's a good start. What else?" I asked.

"You let me chip in on the meal. I don't feel like I owe you."

"Well don't let that deceive you, I'm pretty broke. And to set your mind at ease, you really don't owe me."

She sipped. "What else do you like about me?"

It was the whiskey.... "Well, I really admired the way you pulled on that plastic sleeve, lubed up, and went up my mare's ass to your arm pit with that sonogram probe." She didn't smile back.

The rest of the evening degenerated quickly from there. Fortunately, she had followed me to my tumbleweed heaven in her Volkswagen and could drive herself home. The next time I gave her a call it was pretty clear she looked at her phone, saw who was dialing, and decided not to be home.

When I was at the vet's buying a syringe of de-worming paste for Pete, I didn't see her. I asked the high school student who was being paid to waste time behind the front desk for the summer if she was in.

"She doesn't work here anymore," the kid said.

Later, I saw her VW parked in the employee lot at the Health Center.

Before I get to Middle Fork Road, Frankie calls me back. "You have a way with words, Gabe. I'll grant you that. But I guess you didn't know that I'm living with someone. I posted it on my Facebook page."

"Well, if he's hooked up with you, he can't be all that bad."

"She," says Frankie.

"Roommate, heck. I'll go find another steak."

"Lover," she says.

"Don't try to make up to me now. Just call me Gabe like you used to."

"No, I am living with a woman who is my lover." She articulates slowly, precisely, as if I were a child.

"You've gone vegetarian?" is the best I can do.

"No, I'm out—through pretending."

"Hey, don't get me wrong," I say. "Everybody deserves happiness," trying not to sound too unhappy. "That's what sharing steaks is all about."

"Find an extra one. I'll call her and let her know our supper plans have changed."

"Now you're talkin' friendship!" It's always good to be enthusiastic when you get power-dropped—like, by a son of Prince of Darkness, or blindsided by an old friend. Cowboy up!

I drive on. Flegel's got to be wrong. Conchita didn't kill Sandra—or have her killed. What for? She had no motive. There was a class on motive with the Drummond folks. It was entitled "Hey, Jealous Lover." In the room they amped in Sinatra singing the song, emphasis on "...you were just accusing me of what you're doing yourself..." And Mother Brindle used to say to us kids, "Look at who's pointing the finger if you want to know who started it. In

Isaiah's and my case we were both pointing the finger... at one an-other. So, we both got the belt.

And that makes me sad all over again in a different way, thinking about my brother. Isaiah and I would've made a helluva team if he hadn't been in the wrong place at the wrong time, doing the wrong thing with the wrong people. But, when a cop goes down for good, then the gavel drops. In many ways he was a Brindle through and through. Ike never talked about the others involved, though I can't say as much about them. The others ended up in var-ious facilities, Isaiah went to Canyon City.

For unloading on him they figured to be out in less than ten. Ike figured to be out when the hole was dug in the family plot. I haven't read much poetry after Kilmer's "Trees" in junior high, and something by a guy named Coleridge when I still had a crush on Miss Mason. So I can't swear to poetic justice, but one of them got on the wrong end of a shiv the second year he was inside, and the other wanted to play tough guy with a guard who helped him with his depression by kicking the chair out from under him, or so the story went. Word gets around. But I haven't visited Isaiah for a while. It makes me feel better, and worse, when I do.

Then I had an idea. What am I paying John Woo for? Maybe there's an angle that could get Ike a better hearing in front of the parole board. Sure, a cop was run over, but it wasn't malicious, and although Ike was in the car for a while, he wasn't driving when the cop got squashed. When they came over the hill and there was the roadblock, Isaiah jumped with the bag and a gun, rolled, lost the bag but headed for the trees. He didn't get very far before they winged him. It was one of the others who decided to go all Clyde Barrow and gun the vehicle into ditch just as the cop stepped out from cover behind the squad car. Ike wasn't anywhere near that. But being a Brindle, the only things he gave was a blank stare and a zipped lip—all the way through felony-murder and down the line to Canyon City.

When the system prosecutes, you never get credit for having a backbone. But, by golly, in prison you do. After all, what do you have left when the parole board keeps saying, no. At least Ike didn't crawl, or plead for transfer to another facility after snitching about the guards' and trusties' little dope concession, or the cigarette scam at the commissary. But none of that counted with the parole board.

In a way I'm feeling better again, knowing that Isaiah wouldn't soil the family name. And then, even better, when I make up my mind to drive down to see him after I have a talk with John Woo.

I'm all upbeat as I buy another steak at the supermarket, go to the drive-through for a bottle, then head for Frankie's place.

Frankie has the charcoal glowing out in the back yard. She's an old-fashioned girl in many ways, she likes grilling outside, and the hickory smell. She introduces me to Mindy—short for Mary Crouse. Heck, I know her. I didn't know she was named Mary—or Crouse for that matter. I always called her Chris when I paid for my sweet grain at the feed store. "How you doin', Brin?" she asks.

"Great, Chris..., I mean Mindy."

"You can call me Chris if you want." She pours some iced tea and hands me the glass. It's October, the daylight saving's sun is just gone at six-thirty, we're standing in our jackets. A little late in the year for a cookout, or iced tea. Frankie goes inside and turns on the yard light.

I look yearningly at the bottle. "You used to do a fair fling with the bourbon when we were still going out," I say to Frankie.

"I had to medicate to get through the evening," she says, eyes laughing. "Now, not so much. Maybe later."

"Say, not wanting you to violate any rules, but the guy who shot himself in the leg, did he have a name?"

"His mother probably gave him one," says Frankie.

"And?"

"By the time McDougall checked out the name he gave us, well... ."

"McDo-nothing..." I say.

"Takes one to know one." She nudges Mindy who is standing beside her. They both smile at me.

"Well, goddamnit, I'm not elected and on the public's payroll." Pause. "But did he have a name?"

"As soon as he got his faculties back and was breathing normal he unplugged his IV and sneaked out. Someone must have picked him up, probably hiding out by the dumpsters of hazmat. He's goin' down as a John Doe. I guess he plans to remove his own stitches."

"Be goddamned," I say, sip my tea. The steaks flare. Frankie turns them. Mindy dishes potato salad, sprinkles on some bacon bits for garnish. We all like our steaks the same, so Frankie rescues them after a quick scorch on the second side.

I sit down at the picnic table across from Frankie's plate. She hands me my food. Mindy slides her plate to my side. Frankie gets up for salt and sits back down. She reaches out and takes Mindy's hand across the table. With her other hand she beckons for mine. I'm no dummy. I get the geometry. I take Frankie's and fumble for Mindy's hand.

"Frankie," I say. "I know this is your back yard, and you're the boss, but you're not going to pray, are you?"

"Oh, hell no, Gabe. We're all grown-ups here. I just want to celebrate a moment of friendship."

The moodiness that was chased by the good mood that followed it while as I was driving back from Casper comes again, and for once I have nothing more to say. We loosen our grips, I saw off a piece of steak, chew, and swallow it with difficulty past the lump in my throat.

I get home with the seal on my bottle intact. But I've learned about the dangers of not paying attention to my bad habits. I've deceived myself before with the idea that it would be a good time to stop with the whiskey. Nothing is more damaging to my sense of self-worth than waking up sober and discarding my pledge like a losing raffle ticket, then going out to the barn to look for the emergency bottle I keep there when I pretend to be quitting, or in case Pete needs a wire cut doctored. So, I don't make pledges anymore.

Finagler's glad to see me; Pete's glad to see me. Either one of them knows when I'm lying. I wish I was always that smart myself.

After a couple of double shots, the events of the past day start to come into focus. I feel like I understood something new over at Frankie's. Any day when I can admit that I learned something is an unusual one for me; and sometimes even a good one.

I see that there are a number of things I need to do: First, I put my oxycodone and stool softeners in a ziplock and drop them in the freezer. These are co-evolved medicines; they need to be kept together. My pain has abated enough that it's time to suspend their use. Still it's comforting to know I've got a stash of pills, in case I need them, or they need me.

Next, starting right now, but putting it in effect tomorrow, I'm going to let Leonard Flegel rest until further notice. His finger-pointing has got me suspicious. I believe he's covering for the someone who killed his wife. And, not Conchita, but he doesn't know I went down to Casper to look her up, unless she's already told him. Still, he's been feeling spotlighted, and he should. After all, his ex turned up face down in front of his refrigerator. I don't like to be around that sort of thing—even at a distance.

Third, also tomorrow, I'll call my ace legal team, John Woo, and raise the question of Ike with him. Nothing ventured, nothing gained.

Finally—and it's been way too long—whatever John Woo says, I'll find time to drive down to Canyon City to visit Ike. I won't need to call ahead. I know he'll be there. And John Woo might have suggested some news I can share.

Like I say, it's a satisfying feeling when your plans and good intentions start to come together. But I don't kid myself by planning too far ahead. Life is like taking the pledge I used to tease myself with—day at a time, two days at the outside, and a bottle hidden in the barn.

Proximity

I wake up about mid-morning, make coffee, and call the office where John Woo is working. I get a recording that assures me that my call to "…Belasco, Rambis, and Orchard is very important to us." This leads me to a batch of other numbers including John Woo, so I punch in an extension number which results in another message, this time John's own recorded voice, telling me that my call is very important to him too, but that if it's an emergency, I can call his cell phone, and his recording tells me the number.

So now I have to decide if my attempt to talk to John Woo is enough of an emergency to disturb him while he's screwing the receptionist in the copy room and while all the phones at B. R. and O. are issuing recordings. So many unknowns…, like, does the firm have a copy room? I go with my concept of an emergency, and dial his cell phone. I get a recording…, important, etc., and an invitation to leave a voicemail.

I leave my number and ask him to call me back. I want to say that I may not be able to pick up because I'm dangling from an upper story window of a burning building. But my first meeting with the counselor didn't leave me with the impression that he was good at handling irony—or at least my kind of irony.

I'm microwaving some milk to add to my Irish coffee when my phone rings. "Gabriel, are you okay?"

"Woo. Thanks for calling back."

"Are you in trouble?"

"I'm working on it, but nothing yet."

"What then."

"My brother, Isaiah."

"He's in trouble?"

"He's past trouble; he's in the slammer."

"He's been picked up?"

"No, he's been convicted." I tell him a version of Ike's story, tell him the county seat in Colorado where the trial took place, who the court appointed defender was, and ask if he thinks he could look over the records of Ike's case. "Maybe," he says. "Anything on the death of your client's ex-wife?"

He's got a good memory. "Nothing," I say. "Except my intuition tells me that somebody must have killed her."

His silence tells me I am not amusing.

"Still, fingers are being pointed," I say.

"Mother Woo used to say to me: 'Look at who's pointing the finger and you'll look into the face of the guilty one.'"

"They say that in China, too?"

"I believe they do. But my mother was born and died in Rock Springs."

"I'll be god damned," I say. "I made the buzzer on Sweet Dreams at the Red Desert Roundup in Rock Springs. Advanced to the finals, but Simbee Osis shook me off like a hot turd on a short hair. Small world, huh?"

"Well, Gabe...."

I get it. "Thanks for your time, Woo."

"Call me John. And, I might have a minute to look into your brother's situation."

"Okay, John. Gotta go. I see the UPS truck coming." A lie, but he was getting ready to dismiss me, and I like to be the one who signs off first. A bull-riding thing.

The next day I put out extra hay for Pete and fill her water. Finagler has an old sleeping bag under the steps which he prefers when I'm gone for a couple of days. It's his cubby-hole of a sort. I water him up, give him extra kibble, and get a bone out of the freezer. I leave it on the steps for him to lick and gnaw between naps in the October sun.

I find my brochure from CSP and check the visitation day schedule, throw a change of clothes in the passenger seat of my pickup, and head south. I'll get to Canyon City late, check into a motel, and be right on time the next morning.

On the way south I get to cogitating again. Sheriff McDougall has made his amateurish stabs at pinning the murder of Sandra Johnson on me, and then on Leonard. This is the old guilt by proximity game, a sub-category of a criminal returning to the scene of the crime. But McDougall is no Luke Walter who can solve a crime in a little over 50,000 words in paperback, and do it over and over. No, this is reality. The likelihood of our sheriff solving a crime or having a hot woman deputy in his office unbuttoned three down from the chin for a tease of cleavage is virtually nil. Besides, Drummond showed us the statistics that debunked the proximity theory. Dicky's imagination limits him from going much beyond that. Reality is a lot more messy than formula fiction. Next step is Sandra Johnson going to a crematorium in Montana, while the investigation into her death is in the hands of the sheriff, another way of saying, headed to the cold case file as soon as they find something new to talk about down at Welles' Pit. Maybe a timely tip would help him—if I had one.

The nicest thing you can say about my professional status is that I am a snoop, a collector of privy information. And I really don't want to help Dicky McDo-nothing do something. I need to make a business decision here. In a dime novel I once read, the main guy proclaimed loudly to his pet boa constrictor, "Information weighs nothing, takes up no space; but, it has limited shelf life—it can spoil. Therefore, when the price is right, it should be moved along as quickly as possible. That's what buys you your white mice." At least it was something like that. That paperback came to me somewhere south of Cheyenne on I-25.

Outside of Denver, I catch myself singing: "Listen to your mothers. Pay attention well. Without your loving mothers, you'll all end up in hell. Heed their warning voices when they say beware, and never take that first step down the Devil's stair." It's on the radio. A Halloween songfest—The Monster Mash, Werewolves of London, Thriller, The Zombie Jamboree. Fun. Singing along helps keep me awake—and since I'm alone, annoys no one.

A nice coincidence, though. Mother Brindle and Mother Woo—had they been around, both of them would have said that Leonard Flegel is tangled up in his ex's death, but not so much that he's very worried. Since Leonard has hired me, I sense an ethical dilemma trying to work its way to the surface. But one of the things about us Brindles, we never let an ethical question keep us from making the wrong decision. That's what got my brother a steel berth in Canyon City.

The next thing that occurs to me is that I need to follow out some leads. I need to protect my client, because I need to keep my hand in his wallet, and my reputation afloat a while longer. And I need to watch out for myself. Like Dan Marino used to say in that ad: "Take care of the hands that take care of you." But, if push comes to shove, I'll give Leonard up. That was that "transitioning" that they taught at Drummond Detective. Impeding an investigation, or covering up a crime, is a crime.

As I pass Colorado Springs I make a mental list of all the people who will be subjected to the bright light of my investigative mind. That doesn't last much past the outskirts.

I take the short cut, state highway 115 over to U. S. 50, on into Canyon city, and check into a motel.

Don't Get My Hopes Up

I guess the visit goes okay. I remember, as soon as I get wanded, patted down, and directed to the plexi-glass barrier why I don't make this trip more often, why I can go for months without thinking about Ike. I'm major depressed. I haven't seen him for almost a year and a half, and still we hardly have a thing to say. It would seem that a conversation with a guy who has no hope of seeing the outside again, who is in a facility under administrative segregation, must usually go the way my visit is turning out.

Me: How's it goin' little brother? You're lookin' well.

Ike: You're lookin' better, Gabe. I mean....

Me: Well, I took a spill from Pete the other night.

Ike: She gettin' jump-froggy on you?

Me: She got startled.

Prolonged silence follows. Ike scratches in his thin beard.

Me: So, what you been up to? I imagine one day's pretty much like the other. (No response to the Brindle irony except Ike lifting his middle finger to me from his folded arms.)

Another prolonged silence follows. Ike scratches in his beard, again.

Me: Makin' any new friends?

Ike: Nope.

Me: You were always good at that.

Ike: I don't like gangs. I don't like tattoos. I don't like posse coms. And they don't like snitches, I don't do favors, I don't ask for any. Administrative segregation takes care of the rest.

I nod. There's still some of the Brindle fight in him yearning to be free.

Ike: So, what brings you south?

Me: I got a plan.

Ike: Dangerous.

Me: I got a lawyer working for me.

Ike: I didn't think you believed in marriage.

Me: Not that kind of a lawyer.

Ike: Fresh out of law school. Needing a client to practice on?

Me: A working man's F. Lee Bailey. Said he'd look into your situation.

Ike: What is my situation?

Me: He's lookin' at some angles.

Ike: A pool player?

Me: Not promising anything.

Ike: No kidding. But don't get my hopes up.

A more prolonged silence. Ike looks around at the clock, I think hoping he's timed out on the visit.

Ike: Well, I'm on duty. Gotta go. (standing)

Me: You back in the kitchen, laundry, or license plates?

Ike: None of the above. My four by eight's gettin' lonely for me.

Me: Love you, little brother. Keep the faith.

He looks back and says nothing more.

Guys like Isaiah can spend their time reliving the sequence of events that got them to a dead-end version of their lives. They don't mark calendars against the day of their release. Maybe they look forward to little things, movie night, an hour in the yard, something on the dreary menu which they like, a new selection of books in the prison library. Or some guys become self-educated jailhouse lawyers, file their own appeals, and wait for answers—probably die waiting for answers.

At least a serial killer like Kimball Scott has the tainted joy of his obsessive murders, the taunting cat-and- mouse game he played with the cops to think about. Or Lamston Charles, Jr. who "Lizzy Bordened" his parents because they cut his allowance.

On the way home I argue to myself on behalf of Ike that he isn't an evil man. On that day, which doesn't seem that long ago, Ike was just off on a lark with friends—okay, tear-gassing a drive-up bank unit, busting in the back door, taping up the tellers to a fare-thee-well, and getting away with a bag full of boodle in less than eight minutes, is a little bit more than a lark. Still if a cop hadn't gone down …. That's the whole thing—that and the Brindle code.

The Colorado authorities want something from Ike: want to see him crawl, or cry, or talk about how the three perps were connected to a larger stringer; or, something of the R.I.C.O. sort, true or not. Drummond's ex-FBI video lecturer said, "transition away from anything R.I.C.O." I hadn't had the chance and didn't want it. Us Brindles believe crime should be of home-grown variety. Also, Ike's version of the Brindle code doesn't bend as easily as mine.

Who can blame him when I told him I was going to have John Woo look over the records of his case. "Don't get my hopes up."

Having abandoned my room at the motel, I am driving toward home at night and that gives me time to think some more in between near misses with deer wandering out of the barrow pit.

Welcome Home

I stop in Torrington for gas, to pee, and buy some coffee. I pull back onto I-25, take a swig, shudder. It's about three in the morning, but my cell phone, lying on the other seat, goes off. What did we do before cell phones? People just had to wait. Now, whatever cockamamie idea tickles a person's fancy at whatever time of the day or night—buzz, buzz... on the phone! I don't believe in talking on the phone while I'm driving, unless I'm talking to myself. I've promised I'll never do it! But I've done so many things that I've promised not to do, talking and driving doesn't seem that undoable at the moment. So, I do it.

"Did I wake you?" asks Leonard Flegel.

"I hope not," I say. "I'm on the road."

"You going somewhere? Spending my money on gas?"

"My money now, Len, but I'm coming back from visiting my brother in the Colorado resort."

"The one in prison?"

"That one. The other ones were never born."

"How's he doing?"

"Well, you know prison, Len. It can get you down."

"So I've heard." A pause. "You at a rest stop?"

"I just left Torrington."

"But the reason I called: that guy that you leg-shot has left the country."

Old news to me since the cookout at Frankie's, but I play along. "Really?"

"He sneaked out of the Health Care Center."

"No kidding? Where'd you hear that?"

"Norma told me. She heard it down at the sale barn. You know how McDougall likes to sit and bullshit on duty while they run the stock through. He must have mentioned it to somebody."

"Well, you know old cowboys, pensioned ranchers, and idling sheriffs. If they fart too loud, their wives or girlfriends, will know it before they get home."

Len's version of a laugh.

"So, nobody knows where he went?" I ask.

"Guess not. Anyway, I just wanted you to know." He hangs up.

I say to myself. Flegel must be having trouble sleeping. Why else would he wait until three in the morning to call me?

I call him back. "What are you doing up?"

"I just drove Snickers up to Lodgegrass to get her ticket punched by Lester Woods's horny dingo. On the way home I got to calculating how many things can go wrong. That sort of kept me alert, you know, damned antelope and deer all over the road. I got home, my mind was still buzzing. I tried to walk off some road jitters. Then I thought, you know, that you probably would like to know about your rustler."

"Your rustler," I say.

"Well, yeah," he says after a pause.

"And, if I were a normal person, I'd be in bed, wouldn't I?"

"You're not normal, and I'm paying you to be my second set of eyes."

The sun's well up when I get to Fort Fletcher. I stop by Welles' Pit for some ham and eggs. The usual denizens are there, telling and pretending to believe the same lies, pretending to be amused by the same jokes. Welcome to Hotel California. Flora is pouring the same coffee. But, by god, you can't get a better breakfast—that's not a slice of ham, that's a slab, and the home-fried little reds... oh my god—a cardiologists delight.

I say hello to my acquaintances, but funny, how for some time now, they seem to look away, or if there's room, move away. I wouldn't feel so bad about that if I were known to be a violent man with a short temper, or smelled worse than they do, but they're just worried that I might be peeking in their windows, taking down their license plate numbers when they're parked behind a motel. Ah well, you reap what you sow, and in a small town it's a short growing season from marriage to divorce. But you're careful who you talk about. That divorcee might end up being your sister in law.

I head out to the nature conservancy. I see Pete turn her head from dozing broadside to the sun. I shut down and go to the corral, some more hay and water.

I take a couple of steps toward the trailer. I don't see Finagler. "Alright, you lazy fart." I shout. "How about a little welcome home for the guy who buys your kibble." Nothing.

I hop along a little faster. "Hey, 'Nagler!" On his old sleeping bag under the steps,I can see the part of him that his tail's hooked to, but no wag to it. I kneel down, pat his rigid hip. "What the heck?" I say. I get up and pull the smelly bag out from under the steps with Finagler on it. It was bound to happen, sooner or later. "You gave up on me, old fella."

But he hadn't. I can see someone's helped him along when I tip him off the bag. There's a large dark maroon blot on the dusty fabric, and the bloody matted hair on the side of him exposed as he tips over. "God damn it! God damn it to hell!"

The Mantra

I've done a fair amount of shouting at the moon, when I'm drunk, when I'm lonely, when I'm frustrated, even when I'm sober. The dark seems an appropriate place for that sort of thing, for questions and accusations, disappointments, and sneaky fears. But right now, it's a bright autumn morning and I am shouting, "I'm gonna kill somebody. Somebody is gonna die for this!"

I look down at Finagler's body, bend over to touch him, and it starts all over. "You fucker, whoever you are! You scum bag!" I want to be close to the person who did this, close enough to screw the barrel of my odd-number into his ear before I pull the trigger.

I am so murderous at this moment I don't even want a drink. I sit down on the steps and try to get a grip: to ripple my jaw muscles, grind my fist into my palm, be resolute. None of that is happening; I wish that life were more like the movies sometimes. I feel like I'm peeking through my back door watching myself on my steps and what I see is a broke down two-bit "too-late Charlie" sitting in the sun, crying, raging over his dead dog. Pitiful.

In a little while I'm feeling better because I've started making some plans. Now, the first thing I plan to do is to have a drink of Evan Williams in Finagler's honor and a second one which will seal an oath that whoever did this deed is going to look me in the eye and be informed of the reason he is going to die—maybe even beg not to—before I pull the trigger. I can see it all in my mind, like a movie, close-up and all.

Then I go to the barn to get a shovel.

Nothing ever grew back on the spot where I buried Moriarty which shouldn't be surprising, a clay bank where nothing was growing before. Next to Moriarty's spot I start a hole for Finagler. The clay's hard. I go back to the barn for a spud bar. That helps a little to loosen before I shovel. Pretty soon I've penetrated the crust and things go easier. I cave in the sides of the hole with the bar to enlarge it. I don't want Finagler to be crowded. After all, he's going to be there for a while. I make the hole deep enough that he won't attract one of the neighbor's mutts from down the highway who should stay home but probably won't once they find out that Finagler's gone.

I'm breathing hard when I finish. I put his old sleeping bag in the bottom of the hole, lay him on top, toss in a couple of handfuls of kibbles for the trip. I'm talking my way through this, just as if Finagler were alive, watching me with one cloudy eye open. Then I fill the hole, mound it, because Finagler's going shrink and collapse. I step on the fill once, but I feel the give under my feet.

"Sorry, pal," I say.

I know, I tell myself, this is silly and sentimental. I wonder if this is a signal that I'm over the hill. I don't need signals to interpret. But I snap out of it after I put my tools in the barn. I take my odd-number from under the seat and go inside.

I repeat to myself, "Somebody's gonna' die!" I'm starting to cool off in my sweat. My shoulder hurts. I got a chill. A little medicinal distillate, pour and repeat, two fingers and the mantra, "Somebody's gonna die."

I get to drifting. I remember how I learned the term, mantra, from this hippy girl early in my rodeo career. She spit on me as I went into the arena at the Tulsa Heritage. She was one of an animal rights group protesting "cruelty to rodeo stock." Some protesters were wearing "Save the Whale" t-shirts, others with silkscreened Gray Owls. Another slogan that stuck with me is "Make the next burger you eat a furburger." That one made me smile.

The woman that spit on me was a tall skinny skank—straight long nose, stringy hair. I got close to her, snatched a hank of her long skirt and pulled it up to wipe the spit off my face. "Fuck you, doll," I said. I looked down, nothing but long legs and bush. She jerked her skirt out of my hands.

"You're not brave enough to take on one of your own kind,"

she snarled in my face.

"In the parking lot I've got a black Chevy truck—" the one I hadn't given up driving at the time— "and a Wyoming license plate. Meet me after the show." That comeback—a challenge—should have been the end of it.

"Don't hold your breath," she said.

In the arena, things started out well. I got past Charolais Brown in the first go-round. Second round I drew the bull that was the eventual runner-up for Bull of the Year, Final Destination. I got hung up in my rig, which is what started the problems with my right shoulder. Before I got sprung, he'd torn all the muscles on that side.

In the hospital I was separated from some others in the ward by a drape. I was taped up tight, and half out of it on a morphine drip. I felt someone plucking at the hair on my forearm. I opened my eyes. It was the hippy chick. She must have showered and put on some cologne.

"How you doin'?" she asked.

"Got a little hurtin' goin', but morphine—if that's what it is—makes it all better."

"Think of something nice," she said and then from somewhere in her chest she growled lowly.

"What the fuck?" I mumbled.

"Shut up and think of something nice."

"I'm thinking. Nothing's happening. But what're you doing?"

"My mantra," she said. She repeated it and pretty soon my breathing was in time. I had never heard that term, mantra, before. Then she slowed down the rate of repetition, like turning back the idle screw on an engine, and I was breathing slower. "My mantra," she said. "Everybody has one. It comes from inside. Feel better?"

As I say, I was young then. The morphine killed some of the

pain, if I didn't breathe too deeply, but not my tendency to act badly. I could feel my cock trying to creep. I guess it was visible under the sheet. She reached over and touched the cover, and kept up with the mantra. And then that mantra crept right down her arm and into her fingers, and repeated. Amazing.

I didn't have the mantra technique, but I started chanting too. I looked up and a nurse had pulled the curtain aside. "Pardon me," she said to the hippy chick. "I think you'd better leave."

"We're practicing the mantra," I pleaded from my morphine buzz.

"I'll be back," flower child said, patting my hand.

The nurse scowled.

They reattached some things, tied my arm to my belly, and released me with a hell of a bill after a couple of days. But not before I learned what a mantra was. The mantra master said it gave focus and meaning to her life, put her in touch with the spirit of the universe. I thought that was gilding the lily a little, but I did appreciate that her parents cleared my bill with the hospital and put me up in their basement until I was fit to go to a physical therapist. Her dad moved my rig over to the back of the truck stop and paid a storage fee. They belonged to some sort of cult or something— animal rights, trees, water, air, against bombs, nuclear reactors, pesticides, school prayers-- there wasn't a thing they weren't worried, or protesting for, or about. And they provided their daughter's birth control. I've had worse convalescences for sure. I believe she was hoping to sign me up with her animal rights group. I could have been a spokesman who was a former up and coming bull rider. That would have provided major bragging rights.

And she didn't mind dirty talk, confirming the worst suspicions of schoolboards. I used to tease her when we were doing it in the basement, "I doubt you could stay on a bull for eight seconds with your legs spread like that."

My new mantra: "Someone's gonna die." I sit at my kitchen table and drink. "Someone's gonna die." As usual, things start to come into focus, the result not of the mantra, but the whiskey. Someone felt he could walk right up on my back steps and kill Finagler. Had to know I wasn't home. But, why kill my mutt? Tears fill my eyes again; I'm getting sappy drunk. And is there any doubt that it was that motherfucking Leonard Flegel, callin' me to find out where I was, then…What the fuck is his game?

I decide to go to bed, sleep on it, and then worry about my next move. Mother Brindle always said, "Act in haste, act in hurry; no longer chaste with lots of worry." That would have worked for a daughter, and she was talking to herself, but she only had two sons. Still, in a symbolic way good advice nevertheless, and that goes double when you're two notches or more down the wall from sober.

The Situation

I've been doing too many of these daytime sleepovers after which I wake up at twilight. This particular version has the sun going down, me lurching toward the john, my head throbbing, and my cell phone ringing. I do a needs assessment (jargon from Drummond) and act accordingly. When I'm through pissing, chasing three aspirin with a second glass of water, putting on a pot of coffee, and go to my voice mail.

"Brindle, this is Jensen. I come by yesterday afternoon. You weren't home, but on a chance, I topped off your tank. I hope that's okay. Boss is mad. But that'll hold you through hunting season. You were my last one. Boss said you weren't cleared for credit. I told him I knew that, but you'd be good for it. He said if you weren't, I was. So please send in the envelope. It's in your mailbox. Well, oh, and \$2.43 a gallon. It's all on the meter slip. That's current. He wouldn't discount you 'cause you weren't pre-buy. Oh, and Norma's lookin' for you," he finished. Well, see you on the unemployment line with my trophy elk." He hung up on his own laugh.

Fuck his boss. But I won't let Jensen down. He is one of the decent guys in the three counties. He'll come out in the middle of blizzards, chained up. Nobody on his route is going to freeze. What kind of understanding do you get from a boss when you draw a coveted tag for any elk in Area 35? That's a once in a lifetime draw, and Jensen's been working hard to spring himself for a week or more. I've known a few who drew 35 and just quit whatever job they had; then went looking for employment after they filled their tag, or when the curtain came down on the season.

I sit with my coffee and check my resolve. It's easy to be angry and ready to kill when you're swimming in whiskey grief, the kind that's played over and over on the radio from the Nashville ditto machine. Sloshing coffee on top of a hangover has a way of undercutting whatever you promised the night before. I stand up and look out the back door at Finagler's grave. My mantra comes back. "Somebody's gonna die." And I'm even sober, mostly.

I saw a movie once where a hit man comes to town, rents a room, assembles and wipes down his sniper rifle which is in pieces under the panel in his suitcase, below his clothes. He looks through the sights at the front steps of the train station, dry fires, then sits down to wait with the television on, checking his watch from time to time. Audience gathers he's waiting for the train, and someone on it. I do my version of that. I put my S & W on the table, dump the cylinder, clean and oil it, reload it, open a can of beer, turn on the TV and go to HBO.

Flegel seemed to keep strange hours for a rancher, but he still had a ranch to run, even though his stock was between summer on the mountain and opening the first haystack. He'd already shipped whatever steers he wasn't holding over, but complained that he didn't have a good number because he cut his herd a bit so he could be a hay rancher for the bozos down south. Money to be made. He was always bellyaching. He didn't do his own haying anyway—had it done on shares. But, he was on easy time. Still, he had to sleep. I wanted him to open his eyes and see me and odd-number first. That would help him focus before I splattered his thought-pot all over his pillow.

A second movie on TV, a fourth beer, I still had my mantra going, I put on my dark jacket, my purple Rockies cap, and leave. I can see Flegel's ranch house from the interstate. It's down along the South Fork where his ancestors homesteaded, expropriated, and connived to create the Flegel spread. There are no lights on in the house, just the yard light. I need a closer look.

The highway that the interstate replaced is about a mile west of his house. Government cut out a lot of curves when they put in the four lane wonders, eminent domain, and right-of-way through the middle of some properties. Ranchers tried to drive a good bargain for compensation, but there was no holding back the interstates. I hear the government was planning on nuclear war back then. But that was before I was born. We didn't get the war, so, we still have that to look forward to; but we got the interstates, and Flegel got an underpass beneath four lanes so he could continue to use his ranch road to the old highway.

I drive south on the interstate to the Riddle Ranch exit, turn right on Riddle Ranch Road until I meet the old highway, right again, and drive back toward Flegel's place. I douse my headlights and sit on the edge of the highway until my eyes are adjusted. Then I drive dark onto Flegel's road, and park under the interstate.

Right away, I sense a flaw in my plan. I'm not walking too well yet, and Flegel's house is a couple of hundred yards away. Still, stealth isn't going to amount to much if I drive my truck into his yard. And I'm committed; I got my mantra. A second possible flaw is Flegel's dog, Snickers, who might put up racket as I approach. But, I'm assuming that Flegel was telling the truth about driving her up to this guy in Montana—what was his name?—to get her bred.

I take my time, stop to listen, calm my breathing by repeating my mantra. I get to the picket fence that he told me his former wife, now dead, had insisted on. The gate is open, hanging off a hinge. She had lilacs planted around the south wall. Flegel complained to me a few weeks after I started my spying on her and the tractor salesman, "She says it's romantic and that she likes the bouquet—that's what she called it—coming into the bedroom to offset the smell of the cow shit. That's just busting my balls for refusing to get an A/C, because I like to sleep with the window open. Wonder if she cut some to take with her to the in-and-out motel?" The lilacs are months past blooming, and they're shedding foliage. There's a space between the stalks of the bushes and the foundation. I hunker down there, then settle on my ass with my back against the outside wall of his house. Breathe, mantra, listen. I hear Flegel's voice. He's either talking in his sleep, or on the phone, or he has someone in there with him. I listen some more.

"C'mon, honey," he says. "Do it like you mean it!" Some sounds of effort follow, then "Shit!" Then, "Come back here, the little rascal falls asleep if you don't mean it!" A door slams. "Come out of the fuckin' bathroom and wake him up again!" Pause. "He's raisin' his head, like a prairie dog, gonna jump out and stand straight up." Pause. "You coming out or not?"

From behind the bathroom door, I assume, a mumbled "Kiss my ass."

"Don't make me come in there to get you!"

My plan for killing Flegel didn't involve witnesses. And I've already thought this killing thing through, as I may have mentioned. But Finagler deserves at least a good attempt. And I'm not like the movies where you kill them all. But this seems like a decent compromise. The potential witness self-isolated in the bathroom. I can hear Flegel rattling the door. I crawl out from behind the lilacs. One leg's gone numb so I hop along double time to Leonard's back door. I've been in his kitchen before, but nowhere else in the house. The light's on in the hood over the stove. I see the living room on my right. My mental map sends me south past a sink stall in the hall off the kitchen which I can see, and toward the bedroom. The door's cracked open. Leonard continues pleading, threatening, shaking the door, talking to "little rascal."

I move right behind him. He has one hand on the doorknob, the other on his dick. I press my shoulder on his back and the barrel of my S & W by the hook of his jaw.

"What the fuck!" he tries to turn toward me.

"Steady there, Len," I say lowly in his ear. Pressure on the barrel near his carotid.

"What the fuck!".

"Same to you, shithead," from behind the bathroom door.

"Let's take a walk," I say. The hair growing out of his ear is tickling my lip.

"What the fuck," he says again.

From behind the bathroom door, "Everybody wants to do it. Some just can't get it done." The voice is familiar, but I'm not sure whose.

"Shut the fuck up!" he shouts at the door. "And keep your ass in there for all I care. You come out and I'll bloody your fucking nose."

"Knock it off, Len," I whisper. I maneuver him toward the hallway.

"What the hell's the matter with you?" he asks.

"Can you lock her in the bathroom?"

"The locks on the inside. But what's got into you?"

"I saw your boots on the back step. We're takin' a walk."

"You drunk? I'm bare ass; I can't walk around like this."

I give him a knee on his thigh. "I'll shoot your fuckin' cock off, Leonard. Get your boots on and let's go."

"I need some socks." He stalls.

"You don't need shit, except to pull them on."

"What's got into you, Brin?"

I take a shot through the window. I'm surprised how loud the sound reverberates inside, glass flying, impressive.

"Jeesus, Christ! Take it easy." He's whining like a runt puppy. But he pulls on his boots.

"March," I say, pointing to the back door with the barrel of my gun.

We both hear his pickup engine start. Gravel is kicked into the picket fence as his truck turns and drags out.

"The goddamned whore! Musta gone out the bathroom window." He leans toward the hallway. "Took my fucking pickup."

"Hold it, Leonard. Don't go reaching for anything. Ain't nothin' you need to know in there."

I tap him on the shoulder with my S & W. "Sit down." He is pitiful, naked in his boots, pale as a baby except for his hands, face, and neck. I can't take a second look. He sits down.

"I'm here to kill you Leonard, you sonofabitch! I want you to look me in the eye and say you're sorry before I pull the trigger."

"What the fuck you talking about?"

"You know what I'm talking about. Admit it, you pussy-whipped pimp!"

"What'd I do?"

"I don't know what your game is, but there are a couple of things that you may not touch in my life." I sounded like I was in one of Craig Justin's corny western novels. Had I been I would have enumerated my dog and my horse, and then for authenticity, my whiskey. "You are going to die."

"What the fuck do you think I did? Whatever it is I didn't do it."

"Fuck you didn't!"

"Fuck I did!"

"What the hell were you up for in the middle of the night, calling me to see if I was home."

"I got back from Montana. I couldn't sleep. Like I said, I took Snickers up to Lester Wood, she was cycling... ."

"Worked out perfecter than you planned, huh?" I realize that you can talk, breathe, and that your mantra can go on behind all of that at the same time. I'm not sure how another person can tell when your resolve's slipping. But that's what I think he senses.

"Brindle, snap out of it."

"Get down on your knees, you fucker." I don't sound very convincing. Mostly silently I do my mantra. I hear the words in my head again, the sound is in my chest.

"Brin, you need to sit down. I think you've flipped."

"Kneel, you sonofabitch."

He doesn't move. "If you're going to shoot me, then shoot

me. I'm not kneeling for you. But like I'm telling you, I got to thinking on the way home. Every fucking thing can go wrong..., at any given time. You never know what's comin' next. I shouldn't have visited Lester. I was so wired I needed to talk to somebody. That's why I called you."

"And, I'm telling you..."

It was like he didn't hear me. "Ranching. Take the weather for instance. You got your droughts, your blizzards; then disease, throw in your brucellosis, your scours, your heelflies, your blue tongue, your mad cow. What're they eating? Larkspur, arrowhead—bloated with beetles carving them out. Or your hay can go up in smoke or turn to weevil or grasshopper shit. Then you're short of hay if you haven't read your Almanac and planned for it, so you have to buy when the price is high. If you cut your herd instead, and others do, the beef prices tank because of too many cattle on the market. Then a beef shortage follows, prices spike, but you got nothing to send to market....."

I've heard it all before. He's on a roll.

"You think about some herd insurance, just in case there's an outbreak of something, and the whole thing goes over the cliff, but you're afraid to make a claim for a half dozen steers somebody's rustlin'; that's why the deductible's so fuckin' high, and the premium too. So, you don't. Then someone leaves your ex-wife dead on your kitchen floor. What's next? I'm tellin' you Brindle, its....."

I look at him. Pitiful doesn't describe the picture. Buck naked, but for run-over Naconas, sitting in his kitchen. Me holding a gun on him. Him going on like he's plugged into a doomsday machine. He's catalogued more problems than there are flies on cow plop. When you're imagining troubles, everything is a trouble. And cap it off by having trouble getting it up.

My mantra has faded. Flegel didn't kill my dog. I'm pretty sure of that. Someone did, but it isn't Leonard. So how do I back out of this situation?

Marbles

He looks up at me. "Get it over with. Put me out of my misery."

"It's nothing personal, Leonard," I say. That's about as lame a line as I've ever uttered. "Do you have anything to drink?"

"Why didn't you say so? I'd never steal a man's whiskey. I mean, never! Or refuse him a drink. Is that what this is all about?"

"No, but...."

He looks at my odd-number which I have lowered to my side, and then stands up. "Will you put that gun away for crying out loud?"

I put it my jacket pocket. He walks over to a cupboard, his little pinched white ass in the dim light of the stove hood. He opens the cabinet door. "Will Old Crow work for you?"

I nod. He takes out the bottle. The seal is unbroken. He sets it on the table. "Want ice?"

I shake my head.

I realize that the initiative has slipped from my hands. That's what happens when you start out on the wrong foot.

He goes to another cupboard and takes down two tumblers. He splits the seal on the bottle, pours a fair amount in each glass. He hands me one, takes the other. "Bottoms up."

We do.

"Would you mind if I put on some clothes?" he says.

"Go ahead."

He goes down the hall. I am thinking clearer, but too late. And now I've made a mistake. He might come out blazing with whatever firearm he keeps hidden in the bedroom. He has every right. Home invasion with deadly intent. I can look down the hall from his table. As soon as he disappears, I get up and take partial cover out of sight behind the bulge of his refrigerator.

Pretty soon he returns, looks around. "I need to take a leak," he says when he spots me. "But I can't get in the bathroom. I'll have to climb in through the window. What the heck are you doing back there? I thought you might have left." He passes me and steps out of the back door; pisses by the wall. Some things are just easier done the old-fashioned way.

"I'm sorry about this," I say, sounding even dumber than I feel. I wish those Drummond people had given me a better script. "You have every right—you know—to have shot me." I explain, though he didn't ask, "And, I'm parked under the interstate. Gimped up like I am, you could've shot me in your driveway, for that matter."

"Why the hell would I want to do that, Brin? Besides, I don't even own a gun—if you don't count my single shot .22 . I saw too many guns over there." He points with his chin to the place in his memory. "That's one of the reasons I hired you." He looks at me, head cocked. "Been a hell of an evening, huh? You going to be okay? I'm kind of hungry. Are you?"

I shake my head. This man is loco, I think. I come within notch of killing him and that woke up his appetite.

"Over there, close calls, or bad ideas, always made me hungry."

"You're kidding."

"Nope. Crazy comes in a lot of different ways. Ask any vet."

"On second thought...," I say.

"I did one of those stovetop macaroni and cheese things. Ate half of it. Just add milk, stir, you know. Not bad." He invites me again with a nod. "I'll put some in the microwave."

I gesture toward the bottle. "Would you mind?" I've always felt a man should pour in his own house.

"Sure." He pours me a good dose, a little less for himself. "Then we'll eat something."

"Leonard, I really am sorry about all this." I gesture with my glass-holding hand to be inclusive of the last half hour. "But somebody shot my dog."

"Well, I'll be a sonofabitch." He shakes his head. "Why didn't you say so? I know how you feel. If someone shot Snickers, I'd..." He turns his head back and forth looking for the word; not finding it. "No, that mutt's a pain in the ass, and sometimes I feel like shootin' her my-self. But nobody else better not." He takes the Tupperware with the macaroni and cheese out of the fridge. Something else is on his mind. "How much did you hear?"

"Hear?" I ask.

"You know, from my bedroom."

"I didn't hear a fuckin' thing, Leonard, except you shouting at your bathroom door. That's when I come busting in like a fool."

He knows better, but as Mother Brindle used to say, "one man lies, the other swears to it." Of course, she was talking about me and Ike.

"Would you mind driving me around so I can find my pickup?"

"Whoever she is, she's probably half-way to Billings, by now. Or Casper," I add with a wink.

"I doubt it. We can probably tour the town and find it."

I don't ask who it was in the bathroom that stood on the toilet and raised the window, dropped out, then took his truck. I'm pretty sure Leonard knows where it is, but he doesn't want to go there too soon. So, we play the game of looking here, and there, in the obvious places, the motel parking lots, Main Street, the lot behind the Hide-Away, the feed store, pass the sheriff's deputy and wave nonchalantly "Well, shit," says Leonard.

"Might could be behind the sandwich shop," I suggest.

"I looked back there on the way by," he says. "Onliest other place I can think of would be the sale barn lot. Haven't been there yet."

We go out the county road to the barn. The pens are empty, of course. There are a few stock trailers short-stopped there. Away from the direct glare of the halogens is his truck. "Well, I'll be goddamned," he says.

Yeah, me too, I'm thinking. "Len, I'm sorry," I say as he gets out. "All this stuff going on has got me jumpy."

"And no idea who shot your dog?"

I shrug.

"Well, I know that edgy feeling. But you're the one supposed to be looking out for me, aren't you?"

"I'm on the job, Len." For good reasons I don't sound convincing.

"Get some rest," he slams the passenger door.

I think about waiting to see if she left the keys in his Dodge, but he's sure she did; at least he doesn't ask me to stay. Before he gets in, I pull around and roll down my window. "I'll get the glass man to come down from Sheridan to take care of that kitchen pane."

He gives me a thumbs up.

On the way home I try to get my mantra going again. "Someone's gonna die." But it keeps jumping the track.

And that's another thing about words. Even when I was in high school Miss Mason told me I was good with words, that I had "quite a vocabulary." I remember telling her that words were like marbles, you carry them around in your pocket, and if you get a chance, you have a game. Then she told me I was good at similes. That was a word I didn't know back then. And back then I ran my mouth because I had a crush on her. Wanted to impress her. Now, I'm past impressing anyone, and I feel dumb as a pile of shit.

Sometimes saying I'm going to do something stands for having done it. I'm sure glad I didn't shoot Flegel. He's not a friend, but you just can't go around shooting the first person you suspect of killing your dog. And now I have no idea who might have done it. But somebody's going to die—at least that's what my mantra, which has come back, keeps telling me.

The Cop And The Detective Show

The closing seminar of the mostly mail-order DVD, plus a couple of workshops, which constituted the Drummond Detective course was offered at the Holiday Inn in Laramie, not that there were that many of us Sam Spades from Wyoming. But Laramie, mid-winter almost two years ago, was cheaper than Denver. And I suppose there was a tax thing for Drummond, and a batch of old saws for us wannabees. Getting together in the cold windy town allowed Drummond to update the pictures in its brochure with background of the University's buildings. The correspondence part, the DVDs, the true/false exams in the pre-addressed envelopes, the poorly Xeroxed samples and manuals, were supposed to be "...supported and made concrete by meeting our outstanding faculty with over a half-century of investigative experience, and hundreds of cases successfully resolved."

The reality of the seminar was a quartet: an old FBI guy, an old detective, a retired cop, and a "facilitator." The guy sitting next to me did the math. Not counting the facilitator, and all other things being equal, the outstanding staff had enough experience that if you added it all together, and threw in a couple of cookie jar investigations, you could get fifty plus years. They imparted the lessons of this experience in the form of stories from the field, accompanied by mostly disassociated handouts, and a little finger wagging with dos and don'ts.

But some of the stuff they said made sense. For instance, nothing can replace good old fashioned field work. The other thing we were warned about was watching television cop and detective shows. "They can wrap up a case in an hour—you got your crime scene, your crime lab, your interrogation room. Some of the time your police type detective is standing in front of a bulletin board with pictures and names pinned to it and strings or tape stretched from one pin to another, looking thoughtful, having insights. They use these sets over and over because it's cheap. But cases are solved in the field." That was the retired cop, who added, "Not that you're cops, but you get my meaning, and you gotta know when to transition your work."

That word again. I liked it. Know when to get off the field and go to the bench. And the facilitator—the best thing about her was undressing her in my mind while she stumbled through the professional jargon. This wasn't the first time I had had seen her. She used to sell Cadillacs on late night TV from behind an Escalade and was way more attractive than the distinguished faculty. Properly prepared for her new role, however, she reminded us of the fact we were "private investigators to be," (pending passing the final exam, getting bonded, being granted carry-concealed permits if that was our preference, and so on), and that our jobs would entail mostly information gathering and getting people to move toward a resolution of their problems. Whatever....

She reminded us, again, that a Drummond Detective Academy certificate was a ticket to an exciting career. "That and five dollars will get you a coffee in Starbucks," the guy beside me mumbled. She concluded with another stern but smiling reminder that we would be "...functioning at the pleasure of law enforcement, and you must be alert to the proper time to transition a case into their hands—" that again— "if it comes to that." Practice makes perfect. "The vigilante disclaimer," said the guy next to me.

After my evening visit to Leonard Flegel I'm burnt out on field work. I get to thinking that maybe a TV set with pictures and strings might be a good break, a little pretending. I clear the table and start out with how I got involved with this—dare I call it a "case?" It sounds like a bad voice over to a worse film. Leonard was losing cattle. Leonard to me—no string, just a line drawn between us on a piece of butcher paper. This isn't TV, this is reality. And an earlier line representing me videotaping his wife in *flagrante delicto*. That's what Leonard's lawyer called it at the hearing where I testified. In Latin, that sounds like a whole lot more fun than getting humped by a John Deere salesman and pretending to enjoy it. My gosh, I love language, just like Miss Mason said. That Latin might come in handy someday. I tuck that marble into my pocket.

Then, I ran into Norma Smith, the brand inspector on the morning after my first night ride. A line to her from me; and one to her from Leonard. Then comes the corpse of Sandra Johnson. Line to Leonard—after all she ended up in his kitchen.   A line to the pimply assed salesman. Then, Sheriff McDougall tries to hook me, or Leonard, up with Sandra Johnson's body, but he's lazy and stupid. That line is in dashes. Then, I go get me a lawyer. So, John Woo is hovering, but not really connected—no line. Then I shoot the rustler, identity unknown, in the leg. A line to Leonard, a line to me, and a line to the rustler's accomplice, unknown, symbolized by an X just like in the algebra class I failed in high school. Then I go see Conchita after I find out that she's still letting Leonard come down for visits, about which she hinted she is not very excited. A few more lines.

This is a fucking mess. This doesn't help. My diagram wouldn't help even if I put it all up on the wall, if I had a bulletin board, and the rest of the stuff they use on TV.

There are a few more recent contacts, Jensen the propane guy, Flora refilling coffee at Welles' Pit, Dudley Morton, the game warden, Frankie and Mindy. They aren't entangled in my web drawing because none of them figure as far as I can see. The TV cops get to work from a script. But I'm winging it. And I got more lines than a blue grass band. But it doesn't clarify a thing. Which just goes to show you.

Before noon the next day I decide to find out what I can, amateur forensics-wise, about the shot that killed Finagler. The bullet's gotta be right under the back steps, mushroomed in the dirt somewhere, unless I dragged it out with the old sleeping bag and buried it. I go out and start removing the planks. I made the steps, saved on screws, so that doesn't take long.

From my forensics supplies in the barn I get an old screen for the trailer's missing storm door, lean it against the trailer house at about a forty-five degree tilt, and with the shovel that I used to bury Finagler, I start sifting dirt. The pebbles and gravel accumulate at the bottom. I toss out a few larger rocks and save the smaller screenings in a bucket. I could confuse a bullet for a pebble, so I wash the screenings. The rear of the jacket, free of dust, should be shiny and easy to pick out, even if the front's deformed. The sonofabitch who killed Finagler didn't shoot through the wood of the steps. They don't have any holes except where the old recessed carriage bolts fit when the boards were my horse trailer's floor planking before I replaced it. Norma comes around the corner of my trailer. "Gabe," she says by way of greeting.

"Norma," I respond by way of acknowledgement. "You been looking for me?"

"You going any place?"

"Like?"

"You know, out of the county, trailering your mare."

"I get it, they passed a law against horse trailers. Well, it was bound to happen."

"What law?"

"They didn't?"

She spat Days-o-Work juice in the cheat grass. "You don't make any sense." She wipes her mouth, then picks her front teeth with her pinky nail. "I'm just saying that you'll need a health certificate."

"I'm not sick."

She ignores me. "An outbreak of the strangles. Somebody relayed some horses from Rapid City, overnighted them at the fairgrounds headed somewhere. Must have sneaked them out of South Dakota. Probably headed for slaughter in Canada. They got a crew out there cleaning stalls, sterilizing the water troughs, spraying bleach. The vet had to send to Denver for more amoxicillin."

"Well, Pete hasn't been in contact with any horses."

"That don't mean you don't have to have a health certificate if you're crossing the county line. And that comes from the state vet."

"Whatcha gonna do; set up roadblocks?"

"It's voluntary."

"Well that oughta work real good—'passengers will please refrain from flushing toilets on the train.'"

"But, they can make it compulsory." She narrows her eyes.

"They can try. But me and Pete aren't going anywhere, anyway."

"Fixing your steps?" she gestures.

"Yeah."

"Just thought you oughta know."

"I appreciate it."

She went back toward her truck, parked in front of my house on wheels.

On a hunch I hobble after her. "Norma."

She climbs up, closes her door, leans on her elbow out the window. "What?"

"What about the sale barn?"

"What about it?"

"Well sometimes people park their rigs down there overnight."

"They haven't had a horse sale since spring."

"I know that," I say. "But, sometimes it's a, you know, a relay spot...."

"Gotta go," she says and gooses her pickup.

"Bingo," I say to myself. I stand up and rub my back with both hands. I can't help but smile. I have a good idea that one of my lines on the butcher paper, standing for a string, was just explained to me. It brings back a cliché one of the so-called detectives peddled at the seminar: "Information is like a highway, but there are detours and confusing signs, road construction crews, and wrecks." Well fine, I think, but I'm pretty sure I know where Leonard's little rascal had been trying to hide its head, because it's pretty clear that Conchita has become hard to please while she's bargaining for something, and doesn't like to mix business with pleasure, if I can call it that.

I take my bucket to the hydrant and start sloshing and sorting, handful at a time. Near the bottom with fresh water I see a glint. Sure as hell. I got me a pretty badly mangled bullet. Must have hit a rock straight on after it went through Finaglers chest. My back is aching, but I got me some evidence. Of what, I don't know, yet.

With the steps gone I have to grab the doorframe and pull myself up to go inside. I'll clean up my mess and reassemble my steps later. Right now, I owe myself a congratulatory moment. Forensic Files has got nothing on me. I put the slug on the kitchen table, get down the bottle—well actually I had never put it away—and take a belt.

After a contemplative hygienic gargling of my first mouthful—purging the dust—swallowing, an image of Finagler's assassin approaching my old dog—he might even have known his name, calming him down and slipping the barrel of his gun between the boards of my steps.... My mantra returns. "Someone's gonna die!" Bad enough that my mutt is starting to decompose in the clay bank up behind the corral, but now I have to reassemble my back steps. "Somebody's gonna die, for goddamn sure!"

It's near the end of the business day, but I take a chance and call John Woo. I get the initial recording, punch John's extension and am surprised when he picks up. I give him a version of my dog's death, leaving out my moonlight visit to Leonard Flegel.

"Do you have any idea who might have done it?" he asks. "Who has it out for you? Who's sending you a message?"

"If I knew, you can fuckin' well believe— "

"Now, Gabriel, as your lawyer, I should caution you not to act impulsively." They must all say that.

"My mother, who was a kind soul, used to act—probably impulsively—all over my ass, and Ike's too. But I never heard her use
the word." I hope I sense him smiling. "But here's the deal. I've
recovered the slug that killed Finagler. At least I think it's the slug.
It's pretty badly mangled. But, don't you lawyers know how to get
something like this I. D.ed?"

"You mean a ballistics profile?"

"I guess that's it. You know, what caliber, what kind of gun?"
And then I remember the Drummond seminar, and the pooh-pooing
of the TV shows.

"Caliber usually; gun…,not often. They can match a slug to
a slug, a slug to a gun sometimes—if they have them both and can
do a gelatin firing, but unless a hypothetical gun has a very unusual
twist—degrees of spiral per inch, number of riflings, raised or depressed, the make of the gun may not be discovered. But, just for
an example, you have over a million—give or take— .25 caliber Be-
rettas out there. The brand name doesn't help much." He giggles,
I don't know why. But I can't visualize who might be under his desk
in his office after the rest of the barrister crew has gone. "So, yeah,
I could probably get the caliber scoped. Bring it over. Our ballistics
guy owes us a favor anyway. We'll see how close to free I can get it I.
D.ed."

I am ready to plead UPS or FedEx again, but John goes on. "I
looked at your brother's stuff—not much to say. Witnesses, a dead
cop, two accomplices flipped and made a deal. As you must know,
felony murder doesn't make it necessary for your brother to be
driving the car that killed the cop. Your brother pleaded not guilty,
clammed-up, and didn't try the heartstrings strategy—or argue that
he was taken in by a mastermind. Any dime store lawyer appointed
by the judge could have handled his defense since there was no way
out." We are in John Woo's territory, and he is showing me what he

knows. I don't mind. I'd hate to think that I wrote a bad check to hire an incompetent.

"But times are changing," he says. "They're selling pot from mom and pop stores down there in Colorado. The drug convictions of the nineties are now being considered for early release—a money move, not mercy—and they have to clean out a couple of wings in the prisons for the upcoming horde of terrorists they plan on discovering. Federal grants pay for those cells even if they're empty. That's where the money is—Homeland Security. Federal government will even pay for more parole officers. Not a bad job, benefits and all. And, business is business.

"But parole boards are mostly a power trip. They like remorse and subordination at a parole hearing, a little *mea culpa*. But when they get it, they believe an inmate is sucking up. In the Middle Ages they'd be pushing splinters under the nails of prisoners for the pleasure of it. The records say your brother's been a model inmate. That and a hot shower after sucking up, heck, he probably wouldn't feel the pain. If he'd...."

"My brother won't do that," I interrupt. "He's a Brindle; but not like me."

Woo sighs. "You're a Brindle, Gabe. But what does that mean?"

"It means that unlike me he lives up to the name."

My lawyer is silent.

"I'll bring the slug by, but I gotta go, John. Fed Ex truck is coming."

Brake Failure

The state highway, west over the mountain, is "scenic." That's how it's advertised on the signs along the interstate, hoping to lure drivers to leave the four-lane to pass through Fort Fletcher and drop some money before continuing west over the mountain toward Yellowstone on the state highway. The Chamber of Commerce goes further in its brochures; the highway is called both "scenic" and "historic." Well, what isn't? That's the thing about history and vistas.

Usually over-equipped vacationers, out roughing it, hauling most of the expensive family possessions—car, boat, flatbeds of ATVs, etc., behind the RV read the warning signs about 7 % grades which suggest checking brakes and shifting down. The Fort Fletcher Gazette has a few stories every year about missed opportunities, shredded brake shoes, or even about professionals in the front of eighteen wheels with smoking liners or low brake fluid. The Chamber of Commerce plays along and dutifully mentions the steep descents both ways in their brochures: "Be sure to check brakes and equipment and shift down before descending from enjoying the beautiful mountain scenery." Most do, some don't. And the Chamber revised its brochure when the DOT improved the road a couple of times and installed a "dynamic runaway catcher"—a chute with cables and fancy resistance stuff. But you can't overcome the geological epochs that left all of that mountain up there.

Every summer a couple of the cheap motels are taken over for six weeks by graduate students from the Dartmouth Geology Department. They wear sun tans, beards, or halters, and khaki shorts with cargo pockets. They wield pointy hammers and strange vocabularies. They love the cuts through the eons of rock.

Up on top, the tourists take pictures of the snow still in crevasses in July, and everyone is warned again by signs to use lower gears and to check their brakes before descending. But, as I say, not everyone reads or heeds.

A picture in The Fort Fletcher Gazette last summer showed a driver on his knees praying to the "state-of-the-art dynamic steel bands of gradient resistance," the device which stopped his eighteen wheels loaded with baled hay, and with brakes on fire. A few weeks later there was a picture of a demolished truck, gulched, leaking crude into the creek. That driver bypassed state-of-the-art for an old-fashioned attempt to negotiate "Deadman's Curve." Tally one more for the curve.

The new dynamic truck catcher is an upgrade from the steep cutout, approachable by crossing the yellow line and ascending a hill with a high center of pea-gravel. The high center and grade ascent will stop a runaway but usually takes out steering tie-rods, muffler, transmission, and anything else hanging down. Often tourists, ignoring the signs, use the turnout as a spot for picture taking of the two hundred foot granite escarpment across Mossman Gulch. I learned the term "escarpment" from a Dartmouth gal. I thought she was talking dirty in a flirty sorta way. But expanding my vocabulary doesn't necessarily improve my chances.

Stories about smoking brake descents from "the hill" are always good fodder for the deadbeats at Welles' Pit. So, last night when a hapless tourist in a rented RV managed with brakes smoking, to clear Deadman's Curve and head into the town's T-intersection there was much excitement at the Pit. He'd gone straight into the artfully constructed barricade, yards of stone-faced concrete and re-bar and some potted plants—a "pocket park,": the town's beautifiers called the bumper block. The check cashing store behind was set on fire by the RV's ruptured fuel tank. To complete the accounting, the driver and his wife were killed along with a late-night pedestrian who was getting his bearings before he started across the street.

Living my monk's existence in squalor out at noxious weed estates, I am unaware of the accident until I see the intersection barricaded and smell the cooling ashes. So, Welles' Pit is buzzing. Coffee is being refilled. The one-person capacity restroom in the diner has a line. Like old pilots, the denizens are demonstrating with both hands their version of the careening descent and crash which they did not witness. Bad luck for the tourist couple, good luck for Welles' Pit. The smell of blood, even accidentally spilled, seems to whet appetites. But stovetop mac and cheese isn't on the menu.

At the Pit no one is talking to me exactly, and everyone was asleep when the accident happened. That's how eyewitnesses proliferate.

Shortly the house divides against itself, one half blaming the State of Wyoming for a poorly installed, poorly marked, runaway stopper; the other half calling the victims fools, and worse, who couldn't see in their headlights a 7% Grade sign in bright yellow if it had mooned them. A point of agreement is that the victims were from out of state, "so what do you expect?"

I am making progress through my ham and eggs, waiting for the liquor store to open, and wondering if I shouldn't be bothering Leonard Flegel for an advance against my next discovery about the rustling conspiracy. My cell phone rings. It's John Woo. "Just a second, John. It's noisy in here." I step outside.

On the street John tells me that the ballistics guys the firm uses have determined that the slug I dropped over to his office came from a .44. "That's it?" I ask.

"Not much to work with. You want it back."

"Keep it for me. Next time we get together to talk torts and stuff, I'll take it with me."

"What about the dead woman?"

"Nothing."

"Your sheriff...."

"I think he's too fuckin' lazy to try that bonehead move

again."

"When's he up for re-election?"

I laugh. "You got a point." A beat, then. "Thanks, John. My ham and eggs are getting cold." Too early for a FedEx truck sign-off.

And John really hasn't informed me of much either.

Inside, my breakfast has been cleared for the next customer, so I sit back down at another vacant spot for more coffee. Flora hands me a pen so I can charge my breakfast, but I pay. She looks at me with a silent question about who I've been spying on.

The rest of the late morning is consumed in the retelling of earlier crashes on the hill, near misses, asbestos peeling off brake shoes, broken brake lines, balky two speed axles, ice patches, falling rocks, wild game on the road, and so on. The high spirits inspired by the fatal crash are not cruel, just the giddiness of survivors. I know how that feels. Riding bulls makes you a cow-shit comrade with all the guys you hope you can beat down the road next week. After the show, the adrenaline and codeine, the beer and the comforting cowgirls, make you feel like losing isn't half as bad as it's supposed to be, and winning isn't everything. We were all one big family.

Leaving Welles' Pit, I go shopping for trailer supplies, then go back out to my highway heaven, feed Pete, and start reassembling my back steps. My phone is on the kitchen table. It goes off, but fuck it. Leave a message, I'm just about done. Without steps it would be my luck to stagger out the back door in the middle of the night and break my fool neck.

The sun is slipping. I uncap a bottle of beer, sit down and snap open my phone to see who called. It was Leonard. I call him back.

"Brindle," he begins. "I wonder if you'd do me a favor."

Well, I'm thinking, I did him a home invasion, and I did him a death threat. Possibly a little something on the positive side to prove we're still interacting in a businesslike way. "Depends," I say. "I'm really hot on the trail of this rustling thing. Until we clear that up, no one's herd from here to Belle Fourche is safe."

"Really? Whatcha got?"

"Well, it's still a little murky, but it shows promise. So, what's the favor, that is, if I can fit it into my schedule...."

"I was getting' ready to go to Casper. Then Lester Woods called me. His dingo's knot's worn out, so I guess Snickers is done. He wants her picked up. Says he's not waiting till next week."

Ah, love, the gentle emotion, I'm thinking. "Tomorrow soon enough?"

"I reckon."

"I'll need money for gas, if it's past the state line, and to pay for the escort."

"I'll come by on my way out of town." Then a silly question from Len: "Say, do you know how to dance, like, mariachi stuff?"

"Why? I mean, what?"

"What what?"

"The hootchy-kootchy stuff you just mentioned."

"Mariachi, Brin. The way them Mexicans dance. Conchita wants to go out."

"Len, I ain't been dancing in years. And I'll need a map to get to Lester Woods' place, wherever it is."

"So, you don't?"

"Len, I flunked out of line dancing school for being out of line."

A beat. "Be by in a little bit."

"Give me a beep when you pull in. Then I can let the sentries go back to sleep."

I try another can of supplies, which turn out to be ready-made tamales. I drop them in a bowl and put them in the microwave. During the two minutes I wait, I look out the back door, to examine my handiwork on the steps. I step out to test them. Solid, but with a little new-saddle squeak. That'll go away when they settle. I look up at the clay bank. My eyes fill like a teenager's at a sappy movie. This promises to be a philosophical evening. But my mantra is back to offset the sentimentality.

"Compliments to the chef," I say after burning my mouth on the first bite of tamale. A little cold salsa moderates the temperature. A second beer and I'm well on my way to another nutritious and satisfying home-cooked meal. I find the remote and go looking for a gangster film, preferably Turner Classic and in black and white. I like those smart crooks and dumb cops. But why do the cops always win?

Mother Brindle used to shorthand it. "Pride goeth…." She'd raise a brow, narrow an eye, and Ike and I would know that the only one who could brag or curse in the kitchen was mom. On lonely nights she'd tear up, on angry nights she'd clean cupboards. "What's a renegade from Fort Peck supposed to do?" she used to talk to herself. She was proud of her Native heritage, and told us we'd better be too. There was a picture on the wall taken in Poplar the year she was Miss Indian Rodeo Princess.

The guy that partnered for the stock for the rodeos at some of the county fairs that year fell in love with her, and foolishly she reciprocated. They got married, and things went downhill from there, of course, not counting me and Ike. She quit trying to catch up with Bicker Brindle for the dollop of child support the court ordered, but she promised she'd "go Indian all over his white ass," if he ever showed up wanting to let bygones be bygones. "And at least one of you better know how to write a nice obituary for him if he does come by." That ended up being me, but I never got a chance at the obituary. Still, Miss Mason said I had a gift with words. I could have done him justice. Lying comes naturally to me.

I got hooked on bulls in high school; then I tried to combine community college with rodeo. Rodeo won. And, I keep remembering, an own son of Prince of Darkness put an end to that. "Brindle," I say to myself. "Going over your life won't change a thing. Too late. Your pa's been missing most of your life. Your ma's up in Nashua with a bouquet of paper flowers by her headstone. Ike's in the slammer with his pride, and you're neck deep in pretending to be a detective. My mantra reminds me of Finagler and I'm feeling sorry enough for myself that an after-dinner cocktail seems called for.

Then I hear Len's 'bip, bip,' and go to the door to let him in. He looks around, it's a natural thing to do. But it reminds me that I am overdue to pick up the place. "Sorry about the mess," I say. "But the aerobics class just left and I haven't had time...."

He looks at the TV. "Whatcha watchin'?"

"Not sure. Something BBC on Turner— Petrified Forest, I think, or Painted Desert. I'm pretty much into western geology."

"I don't like educational TV. But you get BBC?"

"No, I mean Before Bonny and Clyde. Black and white, cops and robbers."

"There's good ones in color. Like The French Connection."

"I don't speak French."

"It's in English, with Gene Hackman. But, anyway..." He slides a crude map done with Sharpie on a paper placemat from the Chinese restaurant. "Take 90 to Billings, then zigzag on 87— there's no shorter way—and take the first Fort Belknap exit, then follow my map. That's his phone." He points to a number."

"Long drive," I say.

He slides some folded money onto the map.

"I'll probably have to stay over in Billings...."

"Thought you were doing me a favor."

"I am, but I don't pay for doing my own favors."

He takes more bills from his wallet.

"I'll leave bright and early in the morning," I say.

He didn't seem in a hurry to go, so I ask, "That's quite a drive just to get that nipping mutt of yours bred—how come?"

"We go back a ways. And we kind of trade favors. Stay in touch—old time's sake, that way."

"Go to school together?"

"You could say that."

"As a matter of fact, I just did."

"Ever gone to a class reunion?"

"I got an invite once," I say. "But I couldn't miss my shot at the Franklin rodeo down in Tennessee."

"The class I'm talking about graduated from Long Binh in 1970."

"I thought you were a Wyoming boy, born and bred."

"Long Binh's in Vietnam."

The change of expression on his face, subtle but unmistakable, causes me to change the subject. "Have a good time in Casper."

"Here's a check for Lester," he hands me a completed draft. I fold it without looking beyond his signature and slip it in my shirt pocket.

"Like I said, 'Have a good time in Casper.'"

"You already said that."

"Yeah, that's what I said... already."

It was The Petrified Forest. Why does Leslie Howard want to die? I missed that, and I've seen the film a few times. Anyway, I toast the neatness of Hollywood scripting. If, after a successful career as a range detective, I decide upon a fourth career, maybe the fictional version of my life might be a little neater than what I am dealing with currently.

I wait for another BBC, and I open another can of beer. There's a knock on the door. I take my H & R .44 off of the peg, stand to the side, and ask the obvious question.

"Sheriff McDougall," is the answer.

"Just a second," I say and put the old H & R away. I let the county's chief peace officer in.

"Evening, Brindle."

"Definitely," I say. "Something smelling out here?"

"Not that I've noticed."

"Well, you're sniffing around again."

"Your truck was seen parked under I-25 last week."

"Really? I gotta be more careful who I lend it to."

"Yep, pretty late too. What're you and Leonard...." His phone vibrates. "The sheriff," he says, listens. "Well, I'll be god-damned!" Then, "Might as well. I'll just go straight on up." He flips his cell phone shut, pockets it.

"What?" I ask.

He responds by raising his eyebrows.

"Up where?"

"Another RV without brakes."

"There oughta be a law," I say. "Up on the hill?"

"By-passed the new truck net and took on pea gravel turn-out. According to Betty, a fellow from Worland saw it. He stopped to help. The driver of the RV didn't want to leave his vehicle; he just asked the Worland guy to call a tow truck, but the Worland fellow called 911 instead. That there is what a law-abiding citizen does. Too bad he's from Washakie County. He can't vote over here. Anyway, Betty says according to the guy from Worland, the RV is halfway up, stopped on the high center and leaking fluid."

"Maybe he has a cousin over here who can vote... but who for?"

"All I know is I'm gonna be paying for more overtime. I'll be up all night, and we gotta get Jimco's flatbed up there." He sounds like he is ready to cry.

"Dick, I'm going to Montana tomorrow."

"Fine. Go anywhere you goddamn want." He's on edge.

"Didn't want you to think I was skipping out."

"What're you and Flegel up to that you can't park your pickup in his driveway?" The sheriff is a little nosy.

"Talking dogs."

"For that you gotta park on the underpass? And the night deputy seen you and him cruising late." He narrows his eyes.

"Well, we are having an affair, but…."

"Stop joking."

Then I get an idea. "How would you feel about taking me on a ride-along tonight?" I ask. "If I'm seen with you, my reputation'll get nudged back onto the straight and narrow."

"I said, stop joking, Brindle."

"Serious."

"Serious?"

"I promise I won't grope you."

"I promise I'll knee-cap you if you do."

I chuckle. "But say, Sheriff, when I took a tumble off my nag a couple of weeks back, Doc Rangle had the x-ray guy take some pictures. I saw you and Dudley Morton peeking into the lab. Worried about how I was doing, huh?"

"Wouldn't bet on it."

"I guess you weren't looking for me, then."

Bait worked. "We were there investigating a hunting accident."

"No kidding."

"A guy from South Dakota shot himself in the leg."

"Don't that tell you something?" We head towards his county pickup. "Those jackrabbit eaters can't shoot worth a darn."

He looks at me. "Hop in. Better get on up there." As he turns around, "Can you believe it? Two RV's in a week? At least this one had the sense to try gravel hill after he bypassed the catcher.

Community Relations

Riding up the mountain, maybe the sheriff and I can become a little less antagonistic. That is my purpose, just in case an uncontrollable urge to transition something arises. I don't know what his purpose is, but I figure he's not bright enough to know what I'm up to. We ride. No hurry. I hear about his family, his plans to wrap up his re-election campaign, his worries that Phil Short, a former deputy who is running against him, knows too much— "Not that there's anything to know, of course."

"Of course," I agree. "And it's easy, when you're not humping the burdens of the office, to want every crime cleared up before the weekend."

"You can say that again. Walk a mile in my shoes." As much philosophy as I've ever heard from this man. "But that's democracy for you. At the national conference a few years back, they offered a sensitivity workshop. That's where I heard that one."

"Which one?"

"Walk a mile in my shoes. Like get the other guy's point of view. The lady conducting the sensitivity stuff—that's what they called it, sensitivity—the workshop said it was to deepen our empathy."

"How's that working for you?" I ask.

"Not worth a shit," says the sheriff. "I'm not sure I'd know empathy if I ran over it in this truck." A minute or two silence, then, "You used to ride a bull now and again, didn't you?"

"Oh yeah. But I never got all the way up there with the big boys. Got as far as Frontier Days once, and saw the bright lights of Las Vegas.

"PRCA championship?"

"I was there watching. I wrangled a pair of tickets from the daughter of a Coors distributor. Never rode at Thomas and Mack, though."

Up ahead flares are sputtering, the Highway Patrol pickup

flashing red, blue and bright. The Jimco tilt-bed, already there, probably called by the smoky is also flashing, giving the whole scene the festive glow of an overdone front yard at Christmastime. One of McDougall's current deputies, Norton Higgins, is directing traffic around the flares, just in case some might show up.

The Sheriff puts on his flashers too and pulls alongside. The deputy walks around to the Sheriff. "Where's the driver?" the sheriff asks.

"Up there fretting over his rig," says Higgins.

"How's come you brought Liggy?" asks the sheriff, pointing with his chin to the German Shepard in a cage in the back seat.

"In case we need to sniff some drugs or bombs."

The sheriff considers. "Can't be too careful, huh, Higgins? Keep up the good work." He pulls onto the shoulder. "Got that dog with the help of Homeland Security," he explains to me as he puts the car in park. He grabs his three cell and we get out. "Might as well find out what's going on."

I nod. We walk back and start up the hill. He's grumpy, I'm gimpy. Two fat guys on the highway of life..., helluva pair. Thank goodness he stops frequently to assess the situation. "Yep, sure as heck." He reaches down and picks up an oily pebble. "Those ...environmental troublemakers're gonna... be all over this." After we catch our breath we continue.

We get to the RV. The owner is talking to the Jimco driver. Whining is more like it. "Take it up with the sheriff," says Jimco. I don't recognize him, young, greasy coveralls.

"What's the problem?" asks McDougall, breathing hard, but in charge.

"I need to get pulled back down and get goin', I mean...."

"Let's start at the beginning," says the sheriff. He gets a narrative, takes some notes; notices the man is limping. "You hurt? I'll call the EMTs."

"I'm not hurt," says the man.

Sheriff asks for ID. Gets some. "Maisley Martin," he reads from a Montana driver's license. Sheriff flashes his three cell on the Nevada license plate on the RV. "Your rig?"

"Rented; leased, that is."

Sheriff reacts as anyone would. The man could have been dead, or worse, but not a single expression of this. The way he's acting is like... just let me get the hell outta here. McDougall's carrying his walkie-talkie in his pocket. He gives a hello to Deputy Higgins down on the highway.

"What's up, sheriff?"

"How's the traffic down there?"

"Light to nothin', or a little less."

"Can you handle it without Liggy?"

"Reckon."

"Send him up here then."

"Who's Liggy?" asks Jimco.

"Deputy dog," says the sheriff, eyeing the RV owner.

"He directs traffic?" I can't help myself.

The sheriff gives me a c'mon, stupid look and out of the dark the large German Shepherd comes bounding. Liggy is all sniffs.

"Ain't he supposed to be on a leash?" asks Maisley Martin.

"He ain't bit no one, and if he's on a leash then someone has to follow him around."

I am admiring the sheriff's not-giving-much-of-a-goddamn attitude, and how he's corner eyeballing Martin the whole way.

Liggy goes around the RV a couple of turns then sets to barking at the sewage pump outlet on the side of the vehicle, his tail is going crazy. For a dog, this is a lot more fun than caged in the back seat of a car.

"Guess we better give a look inside," says the sheriff.

"What?" asks Martin. "I'm up here, stranded, and the first

thing….”

"Now take it easy, sir," says sheriff. "Our canine deputy is specifically certified to sniff out drugs and bombs….”

"I don't have drugs or bombs."

"I wouldn't expect you to say anything else—whatever you got…or not."

"You're calling me a terrorist because your dog is barkin' at my sump drain? That's some helluva dog."

"Yessir, sniffs out dope and dynamite." The sheriff pauses to study Martin again. "And he won second place at the cop dog rodeo for sniffing out dead bodies."

"Be goddamned," I say under my breath. True admiration.

"So, let's take a look inside."

"Better get a warrant," says Martin, and sticks his chin out, just a little.

"Sir, now listen to me. Under the concept of probable cause, and based solely upon my discretion, if I think you are a risk to flee, I may take you into custody and inspect your vehicle."

"Do I look like I'm a risk to flee? Up here on this goddamned hill, high-centered, and leaking oil?"

"No sir," you don't. And I take it that I am looking at a case of bad brakes and bad judgment—one or the other, or both. So, I will take your advice. C'mon, Liggy, heel. And, Jimco, Brindle, let's go. I will return to my home, to my wife, and to bed. Sorry to have bothered you and I'll wait until morning to wake the judge to get a warrant."

"You're going to leave me up here?" says Martin, the whine is back.

"If you would care for a ride into town, we can accommodate you at the sheriff's office. Cots are available and comfortable, emergency rations, or a chit to eat at a local restaurant paid for by Homeland Security; if you are hurt, the emergency room is bonded by another grant. You need a change of clothes, God bless Homeland Security, they will pick up the tab at The Salvage Store. This is Wyoming, Maisley Martin, not South Dakota, or Montana, or Nevada. We know how to treat our guests.”

"I’ll sleep in the cab,” says Martin.

I’ve enjoyed the sheriff’s recitation, the little tuck of a smile in his jowly face. There is more to this man than meets the eye.

When we get back to the highway McDougall has everyone pack up, the flares are doused. I get in the passenger side of his pickup. “Comin’ in,” he says on the radio. “Roger,” says Louise. Over the static I can hear her pop her chewing gum.

"Isn’t she supposed to say, 10-4… like on TV?” I smile and wink.

"She can say whatever she wants. She runs the sheriff shanty.”

Look Busy

As I say, that little ride up the mountain with Sheriff McDougall shows me something. My scheme was for him to get to know me, and thereby remove the burr under his crupper; but it turns back on me. I am duly impressed with the skills of the sheriff. All the time I thought he was just lazy, which he is, if the pot may call the kettle black. But there's more to him. The ride back down shows me another new side of the man, the thinking, calculating side.

"Dead Man's Curve," he says as we cruise around it. "Claimed more lives than the cooking at the jail." The bright yellow signs with the Vs pointing left, left, left, chatter by in the headlights. "Did you recognize that fella up there?" He asks.

"Never saw him before."

"He's that same hunter that shot himself in the leg a few weeks back."

"What?"

"Yep."

"Don't that beat the stink off a turd," I say in true amazement. "You sure?"

"Dudley and me talked to him in the health center before they cleaned out and closed up his leg. No I. D., no hunting license. We planned on coming back to give him the third degree." That sounds like Broderick Crawford. "But he gave us the slip."

"You peace officers still do that third degree thing?"

"Just a saying."

"But you left him up on the hill." I thumb over my shoulder.

"I learned one thing all these years that's more important than the rest."

"What'd that be?"

"If you're gonna pickle an egg, you gotta let it sit in the vinegar a while."

"But, you..."

"He ain't going nowhere. Tomorrow I'll have me a warrant before Judge J. is out of his pajamas. Everything on the up and up. And I'll save the money that a night-over at the habeas corpus hotel would've cost. Budget means a lot on election year. That's why Becky spends so much time writing grant applications."

"I'm impressed with your command of Latin.

"What Latin?"

"Habeas corpus."

"That's Latin?"

"I can't swear to it, but…"

"I'll be goddamned."

"You knew that." I smile.

"Yeah, I heard it at the convention. But I was thinking of re-naming the Little League team we sponsor with that. What do you think?"

"I never consult on baseball."

"Oh, our team don't play baseball. That takes some premed-itation. Anyway, it was Becky's idea."

"Who's Becky?"

"Our grant applicator. Ever since 9-11 Homeland Security is giving away money and equipment."

"Gotta be true. I saw it on TV."

"The future of law enforcement is to be ready as a first re-sponder for a terror attack, and while you're waiting for one, write a few tickets, direct traffic at the fair, coach a Little League team, and knock out a few grant apps. But there's a limit. We turned down the offer of an armored Humvee with a roof turret for a machine gun."

"You're kidding."

"Nope. We just didn't have the garage space. An addition would have gone on the budget. Homeland Security wouldn't fund that. Still, I wish we had a Humvee. It would look great in the

Christmas parade, right behind the square dancers on the flatbed from Kaycee."

"Well yeah," I say. "Peace on earth good will to men."

"That's what we are. The peacekeepers. But, that Phil Short…."

"Heck, nobody'll vote for him. He quit the force, didn't he?"

"Don't count your chickens…. People like to vote against a winner just to watch him lose."

"Who's supporting his campaign anyway? A fellow can't do it on his own." I challenge.

"Some outfit in Cheyenne who's hooked up with a non-profit that wants to privatize…." He lets that drift. "And worse. That Craig Justin wrote another novel about a deputy trying to beat out his own boss. Set it in Red Feather but anyone who reads it can see that it's Fort Fletcher. And this is where Luke Walter falls off the wagon and starts hittin' the bottle again."

"Shit, I'll bet Justin's writing grant apps too—a guy with his skills. It seems to be a good business." I'm attempting my dismissive "shucks" routine, with a little dash of "don't that beat all."

"Who isn't writing them these days? Except Phil. He ain't smart enough. But he's got Calamity Jane writing them for him."

"Calamity Jane?" I realize that despite regular breakfast at Welles' Pit there are quite a few things going on in the county that I know little about.

"His wife." He slows as we go by the Vets' Home. "But grants are the future. You got your big ones, your small ones; business start-up grants, invasive weed grants; that character who does the steel drums thing, one day he's a hundred percent Jamaican, next day he's a born again Basque—supported by some art outfit in Cheyenne. All done on grants."

"Doesn't that beat all." In another aw shucks tone of voice. Coming into town we go by the Baptist Church. I ask, "What do you think Liggy smelled?"

"We'll find out. We got that dog because we could, but the handler that hooked Higgins up with him said he wasn't much good at bombs, and just so-so on marijuana. His best skill is finding bodies, but then any dog that can find a bone is good at that. Mostly he's for show. The dog comes out of the back of deputy's car and if people start sweating.... That's what I'm looking for—beads of sweat."

"I'll be darned."

"I'll drop you out to your place."

"Fine."

He turns up the state highway.

"'Glad you could ride along," he says. "Sometimes a man needs to have his work appreciated by more than the crowd in the Justice Center. 'Serve and Protect' is not just a slogan. Sometimes we put it to work. If it ain't too much effort, and it's close to election time." He turns and winks at me to see if I get his joke.

Nearing my place, and against my better judgment, of which I am often in short supply, I ask. "You didn't really think I killed Sandra Flegel, or Johnson—whatever she called herself?"

"Oh hell no." He does a Claude Rains: "Round up the usual suspects." He smiles out of the corner of his eye, slows for a deer standing in the road near my turnout. "You ever in the military?"

"Nope."

"I volunteered. Afghanistan, you know."

"How'd that go?"

"Work details in boot camp. Squad leader's favorite expression was 'Look busy.'"

I smile.

"Ever had a wife and a honey-do list?"

"Not that I can remember. Of course, I wasn't always paying attention."

"'Look busy' is the best way to handle that."

I'm thinking, re-election: look busy.

"Never got to Afghanistan, though. Just Fort Dix."

"Fort Dix?"

"It's a prison. Small time offenders."

"You were in military prison?"

"They canvassed for guards. After boot camp, that's where I went. That's how I got into law enforcement."

"Thanks for your service," I say. I try to sound sincere. He pulls into clay bank village. "Glad to get to know you a little better, sheriff. It was instructive."

"Call me Dick," he says, put's his fingers to the brim of his silver belly. "Be seeing you, take care."

"Say." I hold the door open. "When you get the warrant and all that; and, when you get a peek inside the RV up there, would you mind letting me know what you find?"

"I might. But, a little advice." Narrowed eyes, chill of professionalism.

"Hey, you showed me a lot," I say.

"I'd get my current stickers on my license plates if I were you." All of a sudden he creates a distance that means we're not buddies. "Duty calls." He pulls away.

A Random Act of Kindness

I get started up I-90 toward Lester Woods late the next morning. It's a longer drive than I thought I had signed up for, still, I'm looking forward to it. And to be paid to do it. That's the kind of favor I can shine to. I've never been up toward Fort Belknap. The closest was the Big Sky PRCA at Great Falls. Me and a brindle bull, Canned Spam, earned me a 92. I knew he had to be a lucky draw, Gabriel Brindle and a brindle bull, a match made in heaven. But, in the second round, I drew Horny Harry, and got into the well on the first jump. Fortunately, I landed on my bad shoulder. Might as well keep the damage on one side was how I felt, but I never learned how to ride with the other hand very well, or for very long.

Along the way, some of the cottonwoods still have a few leaves. The golden willows are leafless but bright of bark. Magpies and ravens are contending for brunch at the road- kill cafeteria. And I'm reminded of my ranching days, this time of year a cycle ending, hay up, cows pasturing, the end of a chapter drawing near. It's good to remember the good moments. Because next came opening haystacks and getting ready for the grueling winter slog. If a person remembers all the hard work in life, the failures, the disappointments, and so on, then looking back starts to look too much like reality. What's the point of that?

But fall has a special appeal to me when I could spend an extra hour loafing, as if I had earned it, and not have to make excuses. And there's football, everyone clustered on the sunny side of the stadium if there was room. Besides, the game should not be played anywhere south of the U.P. right-of-way. It deserves its own weather, snow, frozen field, numb fingers, though I never played except in high school. The position I commanded mostly was bench warmer, and I rodeoed on some weekends. Still, given enough time us humans will screw up anything. Football in a dome on artificial turf, wearing short sleeves? But I shouldn't talk. On the rodeo circuit, half the events are inside. Them's real cowboys, son. Where's the sense of that? And, I never want to see anyone get hurt playing football, but there are more people hurt driving home after tailgaiting than are ever hurt on the field. They say concussions can cause depression and suicidal thoughts. Try on a losing season of bull riding!

I veer away from re-examining my life—been down that road before and there's a bridge out around the curve.

My phone is in the console. It rings. As I say, with a few exceptions, most folks who talk and drive are dangerous. But I slow, slightly. "Hello."

"Brindle?"

"Yeah."

"This is Sheriff McDougal."

"How'd you get my number?" I notice a chain-up pull-out sign ahead.

"I called Flegel. He was down in Casper."

"No kidding?" I say—mock surprise. "So what's up?"

"The RV on the hill."

"Still up there, huh?"

"Nope, we got 'er down."

He's not getting the little up/down game. "You and Liggy get to look inside?"

"RV on the outside, refrigerator on the inside."

"Hold it, Dick. Let me pull off the road." I go in the chain-up siding. "Okay. I'm stopped. Repeat what you said."

"Behind the driver's station the RV was stripped, re-insulated, tinned up, two overhead tracks, a cooler unit souped up off what was the A/C unit. Eight beef carcasses hanging."

"I'll be darned."

"Rustled beef headed somewhere."

"How do you know it was rustled? Did whats-his-name confess to get the weight of the crime off his conscience?"

"You're not serious, are you?"

"It's in the movies—usually the third reel."

"When a perpetrator has no bill of sale, no purple U.S.D.A., no brand inspector sign-off—what would you conclude?"

"A perpa—what?"

"Perpetrator. A subject in the act of committing a crime."

"Oh, one of those. Why didn't you say so?"

"Oh, for chrissakes! I just did. But if they try any of that in our county, we'll drop the by-god trapdoor on 'em!"

"You betcha," I say, sounding resolute.

"I called Washakie, Big Horn, and Hot Springs." He waits for me to absorb his pro-active move.

"And?"

"They've had some rustling going on over there. They just thought it was some awful hungry locals. And if Louise had given me the stuff that come in off the satellite, I would have known that too—goddamn her! There goes her Christmas bonus!"

"You got satellite?"

"Betcha, when it's working. What're Homeland Security grants for? Heck, Louise can talk to her daughter in San Diego, and see her grandchildren at the same time. But, like I say, there goes her Christmas bonus!"

"She gets a Christmas bonus?"

"A kiss under the mistletoe from the sheriff at the office party. But what have we discovered here?" He answers himself. "We got us a commercial rustler."

"Well say…."

"Here's the puzzler. There were a couple of quartered up horses in there too."

"Quarter Horses?" I ask.

"How the hell would I know. Not AQHA. Horse carcasses in quarters."

"I will be...goddamned!"

"Never seen a peeled horse before." I hear him slurp his coffee. "I'm holding Martin until he gets him a lawyer with a habeas corpus dingleberry, bail, and all the rest of that before he can walk—if we let him walk. But he sneaked out of the hospital so we may just have to hold him as a flight risk."

"Like I said, Sheriff, you're pretty good at that Latin. But what are you going to do with the meat?"

"It's down at the locker plant. Just the late hunters coming in now. I know, they're not supposed to hang wild game with domestic slaughter. But them butcher-folks can spot a twenty-dollar bill from a mile off. There goes a hit on the budget, but it'll be offset if we get a conviction and write a grant. And, if the judge allows us to donate the meat just before election day, we'll let the democratic minded poor folks know it was the sheriff's idea—and, of course, the judge's. He's up for re-election too."

"Giving away the evidence, and taking me into your confidence. Better be careful"

"Perishable," he says."

"You can keep it frozen till trial."

"Another hit on the budget. Besides, they'll turn rancid. And confidences don't keep well either. Need a lot of attention. And wasting grassfed steaks is a crime in itself. If folks in the county found out those carcasses were headed for the animal incinerator at the landfill, I might as well pull up roots and go look for an honest job."

"Bet you're going be in the Gazette," I say.

"They got a good picture of me and the confiscated beef already. I suggested a headline for them: 'Sheriff McDougall Busts Rustling Ring; Local Herds Safe."

"Be goddamned," I say, even though he's a little ahead of himself. "Did you give Maisley the third degree?"

"This call was a professional courtesy. I am not allowed to

discuss internal matters, still pending. Talk to you later." That chill. He cuts off.

I sit there a minute. This takes a little cogitating. He's got the guy I shot in the leg. The County Attorney will probably offer Martin a deal to roll over on his partners—he's got to have partners—there's more than whoever was helping him the night I shot him. That much beef coming over the hill doesn't look like a mom and pop operation. So, yeah, over-easy's on the menu, and all the sheriffs in the basin can get part of the action picking up the local connections. Elections in November can put teeth into law enforcement and yield wonderful acts of charity. Where was this beef headed—and, hell, where was the horsemeat headed? The hard part, I consider, is always how to turn ill-gotten gains into folding green. That was part of the Drummond course, sub-captioned: "Follow the Money." And, I'd say McDougall is as good as re-elected, or almost.

But, for one thing. McDougall doesn't know about Leonard Flegel's losses because Len believed no crime-solving would happen if he did, except to tip off the rustlers. Len wanted to go "old West"— a cow half skinned, a dead rustler. But he may have hired the wrong range detective. I just don't like the idea of setting somebody up to be shot. I'm pretty sure I hit that fellow, Maisley, as low as I did on purpose. From the shoulders to the hips is a lot bigger target and has the whole engine and ventilation system in it. Knock that out and you got a dead man.

I leave my pickup to stretch and mark some territory, watch the trucks roll up and down the interstate. I lean my hands on the edge of the cargo bed and stretch my back. On the floor of the box are a couple of empty feed bags under the rock I use for a chock, a bunch of orange twine from hay bales. An empty pump can of summer fly spray. My new set of sockets that I bought to change my fan and A/C belts, and then decided to have Steady Eddie's Garage do it instead. I brought along Finagler's old dishes, just in case Snickers has an appetite. Forgot the dogfood. I need to clean this rig out, I think, which causes me to make a mental note. That usually puts anything off for a couple of weeks. Mother Brindle had some saying about the road to hell.... But I never believed in hell. Mother Brindle was enough.

A wave of concern. If the sheriff and the county attorney get this rustling ring truly busted, then I am out of a job. On the brighter side, though, if I get to testify at the trial, talk about my range detective exploits, my reputation will get a goose in the git-a-long. Then I'll probably have jealous wives, jealous husbands, ranchers whose stilted five-hundred gallon tinted diesel tanks mysteriously go dry when they're gone shipping cattle to Denver or Omaha and taking the wife with them. So, the future isn't entirely bleak.

I pull back out onto the interstate behind a Fenster Brothers truck. "If you need it there yesterday, call Fenster." Tomorrow's soon enough, I say to myself. A couple of hours later I pull into a plaza for gas and a guzzle. I hate to pee at a truck stop unless it's an emergency. So, I don't. I think most drivers can't see past their bellies if they're like me, so they piss on the wall, piss on the floor. Just think how much tidier restrooms would be if drivers just pissed in the barrow pit, the way they did growing up. And as far as convenience store crews—not a one will mop more than once a shift, unless someone up-chucks the nachos he microwaved out in the store. I buy a couple of cans of dog food before I leave the plaza.

About an hour later I pull off of U. S. 87 to enjoy the sunset while I kill some cactus.

I give Lester Woods a call. Flegel had already called him, described me and my pickup. "Don't like people driving up my lane," Woods explains.

I tell him I'll be a couple of hours more, and conclude our conversation with a friendly, "Leave the light on, and keep supper on the back of the stove."

"Feeding you ain't part of the deal," he says.

"Just an expression," I say. "I got a bag of pork rinds and some jellybeans in my truck."

A pause. "Well, I go to bed pretty early."

"I'll hurry."

"Do that."

When you take on a favor, mostly blind, you never know what's at the other end.

I follow Leonard's map which isn't hard, dome light on. After the right hand turn at the bottom of the ramp and twenty some miles of gravel I come to a sign on the left which says: "Lester Woods, Keep Out!"

Feeling a friendly buzz of welcome I proceed. His road is hardly a lane. It's an unfenced partly graded two track through sagebrush which negotiates a couple of dry bottoms. Culverts would be useful when the gulches flow water, now they're just shade spots of cottonwoods—but the cottonwoods are shed out, yellow drifts in my headlights. Finally, the track crosses a partly depressed cattleguard and comes up a hill to some outbuildings. Before my head lights sweep his house, a half-dozen dogs are barking around my pickup. A yard light comes on.

Lester, a small man, steps out onto his porch. He shouts at the dogs, finally stuffing a handgun in his hip pocket, and picking up a piece of stove wood to heave at them.

I step out of my pickup. "Am I safe?"

"You're as safe as you're ever going to be." He is pale bald on top, but wild hair below where his hat band would've set. "Come in." It is a formality spoken without conviction. I climb a pair of flagstones to his small porch.

I don't extend my hand to shake his, which he doesn't offer. Then he extends his left hand for an old cowboy howdy—if you can't make a deal with a handshake, by god, don't make the deal. I withdraw my right hand and extend my left.

"My right hand don't work much," he says as I follow him inside.

I look around a neat, under-furnished room, horse blankets on a chair and couch.

"Have a seat." He points with his left hand.

"Nice place," I say. I sit on the couch.

He goes to the switch by the door and turns off the yard light, then removes the Colt from his jacket, puts it in the drawer of a low chest, and sits down opposite. "You got something for me?"

I reach inside my shirt pocket and pull out Leonard's folded check, hand it to him. He opens it, holds it close to inspect it, re-folds it. "Missing a zero or two, but I don't take checks anyway. I told him that." Hands it back to me.

"Well, what then?" I ask. "You're supposed to be paid, right?"

"I'll be paid, alright. And a fair share more than that. Tell Flegel he's on the clock and it's ticking." Then we sit in silence while he inspects me as if he's sizing me up.

"Where's Snickers?" I finally ask.

"Out in the whorehouse," he says, without a hint of a smile.

"Leonard must like your dog."

"A champion."

I nod.

"Can turn a team penning into a stampede."

I nod.

"Put him on a steer and he won't quit till you beat him off."

I nod.

We sit a while.

"Once a couple of winters ago one of my cows got out down by the neighbor's reservoir. I knew the fence was flat. Should have fixed it. But what am I s'posed to do with only half a wing on my right side. Anyway, I rode down on my X-pro with Curt. Sent him to put the cow back over the wire; then I was gonna prop it up."

Lester seems to be warming—nothing like a good story.

"Got 'er done, huh?"

"Cow back-pedalled onto the ice, Curt right after her. She fell through."

I wait, then, "What happened?"

"I had my X-pro chained up, all four, so I hobbled out on the edge of the ice, roped the cow, tied off the rope on my tow bar and dragged her out."

"What about Curt?"

"He came out with her; still had ahold of her ear." A smile comes, leaves.

"Well, if I can get Snickers, I'll be on my way."

"Ain't spending another winter like that. I was by myself. But, I'm getting too old. And I can't leave the place if I need to. Someone's got to feed. It ain't easy. Never was. So, I got me a fella hired for this winter."

"Sounds like a good idea."

"He ain't worth a shit, though. I don't speak his lingo. He don't speak mine. He's hiding out, so I don't have to pay him much. But he knows which end of a pitchfork is the working end."

"Good to have someone around. You're a long ways from no-where out here."

"Make a trip in for my government check once a month. As far as the VA knows I'm homeless with a post office box in Ft. Bel-nap." He looks into the shadow corner. "Fucking VA.... Will you take a drink?"

"I'm driving."

"Who's gonna know? I always drive better after a couple."

He goes to the cupboard, removes two glasses, sets them on the table, then reaches a bottle of Jim Beam, which he clamps be-tween his knees in a semi-squat while he uses his left hand to twist the cap. He pours without ice, hands me a glass, downs his, sets the bottle on the chest, cap beside it. I'm usually not a sipper, but I sip. He pours himself another.

"Yep, Curt's earned himself a reputation."

"I'd like to see him." How can I deny it? The whiskey tastes good, that little smile that tickles just under the ribs. Someone told me that was your liver complaining but I don't believe it. "Was he one of the ones that greeted me?"

"Might have been," he says. "I can't tell them apart without looking real careful. So, I video-tape 'em."

I almost laugh, but Lester doesn't seem like the joking type.

"Made me a set up in the whorehouse. Wanta watch a cassette or two?" He looks at my glass. "You ain't drinking."

"You threw Snickers into a pen with, what, how many dogs?" I feel I oughta look out a little bit for my client's bitch.

"What does it matter? They're brothers, except for her. Like my kin used to say down in Carolina country. All in the family. May the best man win."

I'm thinking Darwin of a sort while he pours to refresh my whiskey.

"So, you come from Carolina?"

"Hell no! That's just a saying. Lingo I learned from ignorant hillbillies. Anyway, in the Army, you find your own."

"Never made it that far," I say, hoping he'll change the subject.

"That's how come I got to know Lilly Lenny."

"Flegel—you call him Lilly Lenny?" I shouldn't have smiled.

"He didn't have much of a taste for killing when he fell out of the back of that C-130. But we got him straightened out. We explained to him that we were in a war."

"Well, you know Lenny," I say, and try a segue. "So, winter's pretty tough up here, huh?"

"Ever kill anybody?"

"Not that I know of."

"Well, you'd have no idea then."

"Probably not."

"But enough about killing. It's something you don't get over, even if you want to. It hides in some places and touches you in others. But like I say, enough."

I nod, study my tumbler, whiskey in the bottom. I look around his place again, trying to come up with a good topic so I can leave on an upbeat, away from killing and dog breeding. "How far are you from Canada?"

"Forty miles as the crow flies, back roads."

We fall to silence again. I finish my whiskey.

"Got a coupla good videos." He makes a piston-like gesture with his left hand.

"I should be going," I say.

"Flegel liked my movie shows. I swapped him one. I like the peeking Tom style on his. Got someone to film his wife through a bedroom window."

"No shit?"

He pours another couple of fingers worth in the bottom of my tumbler. Nothing like a good host to encourage my sociability.

"How's she doing?" He asks.

"Who?"

"His wife."

"I wouldn't know. I believe they're divorced."

"Is that a fact." There's no commitment, no surprise.

We sit. I look around again. He eyeballs me. "Well, she was a Montana woman." Pause.

"Curt's a good name for a dog," I say.

"Real name's Curtis," he says.

"Family?"

"Nope. After Curtis LeMay,"

I can't help it. I laugh. He doesn't.

"If they'd a bombed them gooks and dinks back into the Stone Age the way LeMay wanted, I wouldn't had to go over there, and I might have two arms to work with. I'm a right-hander. Ever tried to scratch your ass with your left hand?"

I'm thinking cause and effect. That and the double belt of whiskey—I stumble. "You and Leonard were over there together."

"Over where?"

"Vietnam. Long Binh."

"So, he already told you that?"

"Sorta."

"Yeah. We were in the stockade."

"The stockade?"

"They said we had gone off the reservation."

"AWOL?"

"Oh, hell no. That we had been doing some unauthorized reconnaissance. Night missions."

"Leonard didn't say..."

"Them R.O.T.C. pussies—second louies—fresh in country. They read us Article 3 of the Conventions, like they had the fucking gospel. Like I say. It was a war. People get killed...and other stuff." I study my glass.

"You ever heard of Lieutenant Calley?" he asks.

"Nope."

"Don't matter," he says. Drink up," "I'll go get Leonard's bitch." He stands. "What's her name again?"

"Snickers." I follow.

"No kind of name for a dog. Hard one to remember. Maybe that's why she don't come when I call her. And I don't think she's dead. Like we used to say over in 'nam. When they're quiet, they're either hiding or dead. I just drown the pups that don't look like they'll turn out. Amounts to the same thing. Saves dogfood. Keeps the place tidy."

I follow him.

Out at his dog pen, Lester puts on a glove, grabs Snickers by the scruff and puts her in my front seat. She is subdued but snarling. I thank him for his hospitality.

"Come again," he says.

"Well sure, when I'm up this way."

"Or I'll come see you." He heads for his house.

As I get to highway 87, I say to myself, I thought Woods said he couldn't leave the place. Guess he was just talking. Ranchers are always belly-aching—can't get good help, government is screwing them while they're compensated for predation and stock lost to snowstorms, and they drive tinted discounted diesel meant for agriculture in their crewcab pickups. None of those rackets worked for me when I took my short turn at ranching. Mother Brindle warned us early on, "Gotta have money to make money, and poor people have poor ways." That advice didn't help Ike or me to make wise career choices. But she wasn't one to withhold a compliment. She said to me, just before she passed: "I feel I've succeeded since only half of my kids are in jail! And... Thanks for stopping by." The next morning she was gone.

This back-pedaling on memories while I'm looking into the tunnel of my headlights is starting to get me down. I pull off the highway. Plus, Lester's liquor on an empty stomach has gone to my head, through my kidneys, and putting a bulge in my bladder, if my map of internal organs is accurate. I leave the pickup idling and let Snickers out while I pee. When I try to get her to jump back in, she climbs under the truck. I thank my 16-inch rims and almost new tires for the clearance that allows me to slide half-way under with the free penlight the bank handed out last year. She keeps backing away.

I get a surprise flashlight in my face. "Trouble with your drive shaft, or something?"

"Dog's hidin' from me" I say, shading my eyes. "Won't come out."

"I'll get her from the backside." Samaritan kneels.

Snickers turns to bite him. I grab her by the scruff. "Got her." I start backing out.

When I stand with Snickers he's halfway to his pickup.

"Thanks," I say.

"Glad to be of help," he says, gives me a bip as he pulls across the rumble strip.

Now that's the western way, I say. Stranger having difficulty late at night, stop, solve the problem, on your way. A random act of kindness. The likelihood of someone showing up in the nick of time. This might be a streak of luck starting. I felt that same way when I rode Bean Burrito to an 89 up in the Matthew Knight Arena in Eugene. That streak lasted all the way through the semis. That's the thing about streaks. You only know you've had one when you look backwards after it's over. And that's the worst time, because when you're looking in that direction, you can't see what's coming at you.

Something New To Consider

I'm feeling relaxed. Driving. Thinking. I reach over and lay my hand beside Snickers who has climbed from the floor to the passenger seat. She's a smart dog and can understand that I am not like Lester Woods, or Leonard Flegel. She starts to shed her worries. Human-dog companionships are on a sliding scale from blue-hair ladies with handbag Chihuahuas who chirp "come and kiss mummy's face" just after they have licked their privates, to those who set Pit Bulls on one another to fight to their deaths. Lester Woods might not start a dog fight, but he wouldn't break one up either; he'd just videotape it. A moment's thought puts me on the scale as a lonely guy, wanting to be adopted again, by a dog. I whistle a little to move my thoughts away from Finagler, but my mantra's in the background. I touch Snickers' nape, give it a scratch.

I pull into a motel in Billings. As I enter the office, I catch the night clerk making a plunge with his pinky into his ear canal. He examines, rolls the result against his palm as he comes forward from a small space where he seemed to be watching TV. With the other hand he slides a clipboard with a registry form on it and hands me a pen. I sign and ask if his motel is "dog friendly."

"Not really, why?"

I was going to say, something smart, and asinine, but I'm tired. "No reason, I'm travelling alone." I pay cash. "Where's the ice machine?" He hands me a map of the motel and indicates a breezeway.

I take my key, the map and return to my pickup, then find my way to my room. I carry in my doubled shopping bag Walmart designer luggage containing my clean shorts and bottle Evan Williams, and my odd-number S & W with the webbing belt rolled around it. Before the ice machine, and since I figure the night clerk has settled back to watching the TV, I go out to my pickup again, put on Snickers' collar and knot a piece of binder twine under it. I reach into the back of my rig to get Finagler's dishes and a can of dog food. Then I figure that being in the big city I'd better lock up. I go for my new sockets, shift the feed bags around, but the sockets aren't there. Sonofabitch!

Conclusion: the fellow who stopped to help me by the side of the road while I was halfway under my truck saw my socket set, nice and shiny in the beam of his flashlight, and in the best cowboy ethical way stole 'em. Mother Brindle's caution comes back. "Don't trust nobody. Particularly if he's friendly and helpful, and is carrying a Bible." The Samaritan wasn't carrying a Bible. But two out of three.

I enter my room, feed and water Snickers who's in no mood to eat at the moment. I find a BBC film, nothing heavy or arty. Something with Dana Andrews. I'm usually a straight up drinker, but wanting the full benefit of my motel stay I get a plastic bucket of ice at the machine, then break open the bottle and get settled for the night.

Not quite. My cellphone goes off. I look at the number. It's Flegel. "What's up Leonard?"

"Where are you?"

"Billings. Like I told you I would be. It's late and I'm tuckered out. I need a good night's rest. I'm at the Cottonwood Motel; not a tree in sight."

"You got Snickers?"

"Oh yeah."

"Is she bred up?"

"I didn't ask her."

"Well, does she look bred up?"

"She looks a little worse for the wear."

"She's bred up," concludes Flegel.

Not necessarily by Curt, I think. But all in the family. "You keep in touch with this Woods guy, huh? He's an odd one."

"Since we mustered out. His dog Hamstring was recommended to me. So, I took Snickers up there while I was passing through. But Hamstring had died. He suggested Curt."

"So, you've been eye to eye with Lester Woods recently?"

"Oh yeah. Long enough to drop off Snickers, and get out of there. He's still nuts."

"You said 'passing through.' On your way to where?"

"Just a saying. You know, in other words, not staying long."

"Well, thanks for sending me."

"Did he start in with the war?"

"Oh yeah. And some dog stories."

"Well, as I said, he promised Hammy, but he said Curt was just as good."

"You get what you get."

"That's for damn sure. And, I guess I don't have room to talk."

"He didn't have much good to say about second lieutenants."

"That again. But nobody cared for the R.O.T.C. ninety-day-wonders or the mama's boys out of O.C.S. Did you stay long enough for him to go off on agent orange?"

"Missed that story." I was hoping to get off the phone.

"I need to get some sleep, Len."

"Yep."

"Will you be back tomorrow?"

"I plan on it."

"See you then."

"By the way, Woods wouldn't take your check. And he said you owed him more... in cash."

"That's between me and him then, next time I'm up in that direction."

"Just looking out for my client."

"See you tomorrow." He repeats and hangs up.

Snickers eats a small chunk of dog food. Beef, the can says.

But it's a Canadian product—who checks the ingredients—there or here? I take her on the twine leash out behind the motel. We come back. Both of us have a drink—water and 86, respectively. She circles, sniffs, down at the end of the queen-sized double. Makes me think again of Finagler, sneaking up on the bed after I was asleep. Waste not, want not, Mother Brindle used to say, so I tip the rest of my double up, do a swish and gargle for the sake of dental hygiene, and swallow. I turn off the TV. And we go to sleep.

I have a little breakfast in a joint where a Bible passage on a card comes with the biscuits and gravy. The meal isn't that good to begin with. Why ruin a poor effort with a penny homily? I drive a couple of hours, Snickers is settled on the passenger seat. I pat her head from time to time. But I'm wondering why Flegel would even keep in touch with a fellow almost in Canada and his group of heelers. And why he would drive five hours just to drop her off along the way to be bred. And still, along the way to where? Well, none of my worry. They say the bonds you form in the military last a lifetime. Loneliness afflicts the species. Same reason I stopped by the old bull-rider who had Petunia sold and loaded. Timing. Things are all lined up waiting to happen—trouble is, we don't know what they are.

We come to Sheridan, then I cruise on down past Fort Fletcher before eleven in the morning; cut back direct to Flegel's ranch house turn-off from the old highway just as Norma Smith is leaving. Under the interstate, facing opposite directions, we stop in the shade. I nod a greeting, "Norma."

She spits. "Gabe." Wipes her mouth, uses her pinky nail to clean her teeth.

A beat.

"Well, that's most of the news," I say.

"You don't make any sense."

"I sure hope not."

"Gabe," she says by way of taking leave, shifts her chew, bites down and is gone.

"See you, Norma," I say to the spot she left, and pull onto the gravel beside Leonard's house.

Inside, Snickers sniffs around, gets her bearings. Leonard seems mostly unconcerned, except that she's back again. I scratch Snicker's back but not long. Bending over makes me light-headed.

"We got to know one another," I say.

"You and Lester Woods?"

"No, me and Snickers. Once she gets used to you she's kind of a sweetheart."

"Coffee?" he asks

"Gotta go," which isn't true.

"Not yet," he says. "Moved the cows down closer to the stack by the creek last week."

"Yeah, I know."

"We lost more steers last night."

"What?"

"Yep," he says. "Three gut piles, hides, heads."

"Be goddamned," I say.

"Right beside the ruts to the stackyard. You tell anyone I was going to Casper?" he asks.

"Nope. But the Sheriff called me after he called you to get my number. And, did you tell anyone you were moving your herd."

"Nope." Narrows the eye. "Somebody's scoping us."

I nod.

He refills the coffee. "Ever mix business with pleasure?"

"I figure it's nobody's business what gives me pleasure." I give him just a twitch of smile.

"I see what you mean."

"Better go." I get up. "I didn't sleep well last night. It's about my nap time."

"You riding herd tonight?"

"Don't think I will. Those steak thieves will probably let it rest, wait till we relax and look the other way."

He sighs. "Well, you're the detective, but we gotta catch those sons-o-bitches."

When I get back to bentonite ranch, I feed Pete, water her. She was running low but not out on either score. And she's getting a little roly-poly. I'm not kidding about the nap. When a person prioritizes—what comes first, what comes next—it leads to an ordered life. After I wake up, I back around to my horse trailer, drop my tail gate, hook up. I pull an empty feed bag out from under the rock and start stuffing the trash in it, continue in the cab on the passenger side.

And this reminds me of my socket set, which reminds me of Finagler, because his food dishes are there. My philosophical insight is that all events are connected, and we who are afflicted with consciousness are given the job of figuring out how. If angry and blue can be combined, that's where I land. It's disturbing when the boundaries of your life get stepped on. Then I consider it may be that my blood sugar is low. I go back inside to the kitchen, then to the pantry where I consult with the cook and decide on some Van Camp's. I turn out the can into a bowl and put it in the microwave. Then, I notice that some stuff in the all-you-can-eat salad bar in the bottom of the fridge is not fresh, again. I make a mental note to clean out the refrigerator. I remove the last beer, find some crackers in the cupboard. "Bonnie, petite!" someone used to say on the tube.

I by-pass the news on TV—I don't want to know—but I can't find a BBC flick, so I go to the radio. How many times, how many ways can the same tune get recorded? Fort Fletcher's local station was bought by some company in Missouri whose media skills and musical tastes are limited to subscribing to a satellite feed.

I pick up my dish and spoon. I must have a talk with the kitchen staff about the mess in the sink! I go out to the pickup and get my odd-number, clean and oil it on the kitchen table, replace the cartridges. While I'm at gun maintenance, I take down the H & R from the peg. I'm emptying the cylinder, and I'm a double sono-fabitch! One chamber has a fired brass, a pin pock in the primer. Some bastard fired my gun. Someone came in my house took my gun down and fired it!

One, two, three it comes, even in my lame brain. Finagler got shot. John Woo's ballistics guys determine the slug I recovered to be a .44. And there's one empty brass in the H & R's cylinder. Some bastard shot my dog with my own gun! Behind basic logic comes mantra, amped up—"Somebody's gonna die! And that's a fucking promise."

I don't know whether to punch a hole in the Masonite wall with my fist, or have a shot of whiskey. So, I do both. Later, I'm drinking with my left hand, soaking my right hand in the sink with dirty dishes and ice cubes, contemplating a momentary wave of sympathy for Lester Woods, when my phone goes off. It's on the charger. I dry my hand. "What?"

"Gabriel?" Could be the sheriff, because only my mother and a couple of groupies ever called me Gabriel.

"Who is it?" I was already pretty sure it wasn't my mother.

"Sheriff McDougall. Got a minute?" An unusually soft tone for the chief law enforcement officer of the county.

"Yeah."

"Well, elections are coming. It's the last push. Everybody's got their yard signs out. Everybody's done the candidate forums, the interviews. You know the school board, the cemetery district and so on."

"Yep," I say. "But I'm glad you called because I've been meaning to ask: who's the best candidate for the cemetery district?"

"Nobody's running against Betson."

"That's who's running for the district?"

"Gabriel. I need a favor."

"Boy, I'm glad you steered me away from a bad choice on the cemetery district."

"Do you always do this to your friends?"

I didn't realize we were friends, but I say, "Well Dick, that's what friends are for."

"Can I ask you for this favor, or should I write you a ticket for not having the current tags on your license plates?"

"Ask away, Dick. And thanks for the reminder about those tags. I got 'em, I just haven't put them on."

"I've come up with a little plan that's gonna push my campaign over the top—I think."

"Well, that's good."

"You know Phil Short's running."

How could I not? Sheriff mentioned it the other night on the ride along. Lots of yard signs. But nothing in the published stuff except suggestions that something was rotten in the sheriff's office. "Yeah."

"Were you ever married?"

"Not that I can remember. I told you that before." I'm getting annoyed.

"Well, if you were you'd know you give your last best shot at an argument as you go out the door."

"The last word," I say.

"Yeah."

"Well, I got wind of the fact that Short may to do some—what do you call it—exposé just before election day. That's what you call it, right?"

"I guess. A cheap shot from the underside."

"Yeah, like that. The gal I got planted in his circle says he's carryin' around a brief case full of papers he copied when he got wind I was going to fire him, the bastard. But he quit before I could."

"And?"

"Counter punch."

"Go for it," I say. Family fights are the most interesting.

"The old one—two; and here's where you come in. While I'm out solving the death of Sandra Johnson, you get your crew out to put up yard signs. We're runnin' short of time, but I think we can do it."

This "we" thing really bothers me. I wonder if he has a frog in his pocket. "Put up your own yard signs, Dick. I don't have a crew."

"No, I mean in yards where Short has signs."

"Those aren't your friends, Dick. And if you need a crew, you hire a crew. Cowboy up. And I don't suppose the folks that own those yards want me putting up your signs in them. Is it too late to write a grant?"

"Signs are signs. What do they care? Every spot, as much as you can, where Short has a sign gets a new sign. It says, 'Don't sell yourself Short on law enforcement—re-elect Sheriff McDougall.'"

I like the slogan but, "I don't want to get involved," I say. "I could get myself arrested for trespassing."

"Not while I'm sheriff."

"I could get myself shot or dog-bit."

"I doubt it."

"Gotta go." I hang up.

This is another example, I say to myself, of how things come up. You don't expect them. They show up anyway. I was focused on my mantra fifteen minutes past, promising Finagler some vengeance, and now I got something new to think about. Not to mention, I have to keep stringing Leonard along toward another payday.

And I didn't lie to him when I told him I wasn't planning on going riding in the dark tonight. But I just changed my mind.

Take A Deep Breath

My plan is to saddle Pete, trailer her down by the bridge to the wide spot on the county road where the kids park to spark. Then, I'll go through the cottonwoods and willows by the creek and come up on the backside of Leonard's stackyard. I know the layout roughly because one spring I pastured Moriarty there.

Earlier, I'd recollected one of the things emphasized at the Drummond seminar. Don't tell anybody your business. So, again, my little lie to Leonard about not riding tonight was flim-flam I hadn't planned on—but it'll work. And that's good advice in general. Heck, Mother Brindle taught Ike and me that same lesson for all time. She said, if it looks too good to be true, it probably is. We should have known something was up when Mom called us to breakfast that day. She never cooked breakfast, except for herself, and that was cigarettes and coffee. She said she was turning over a new leaf, but, no. It was salt in the sugar bowl and Roarin' Rick's Hot Sauce in the oatmeal on April Fool's Day. Mom got a laugh at our expense. "You fell for it," she said. "It's how things taste, not how they look, that counts. Use that Indian savvy in your lives!" Ike should have paid more attention, and I just barely passed grade on the trickery scale. But for now...

I'm set up with Pete on the edge of the cottonwoods. Got my black parka on and my balaclava. It's chilly enough for gloves, but gloves and the trigger guard of an S & W are incompatible. I plan to keep my hands in my pockets as much as possible. The odd-number is in my cargo pouch on the right, extra shells just in case a war breaks out, new digital camera, which I think I know how to use, in my lefthand warmer pocket. I'm starting to feel an edge of edginess around the edges, the same feeling I used to get walking through the arena before the rodeo. Everything would be calm, but 8 seconds of hell was about to break loose—or maybe not. That wasn't the right time to start thinking about a different career. I had to go out the other end of the tunnel. That was a trait that Ike and I had—make a decision, follow through. Mother Brindle also taught us that. Later was soon enough to find out if you'd made the right choice. Whatever decision you make, play it out to the last card. Probably one of the reasons she never let my father ever come back. She could have used a little help with Ike and me. But the decision was made; and only one of us ended up in jail.

I'm starting to get to like this Mickey Spillane version of my life. If I finesse the rustling deal—looky there, that's me, the guy standing behind the sheriff while he goes on about making the arrests—partnering up, so to speak. Transitioning like the Drummond folks put it—always adding, "a cordial relationship with law enforcement is essential." Then, as I have considered before, the clients will come knocking, maybe. No way to know if we'll ever get to that stage, or if during election season the sheriff won't merely want to shine the light on himself. Still, I can see the advantage of becoming part of the Sheriff McDougall re-election team—if I can keep it cordial. Maybe I should take him up on his offer. I'll give it some more thought.

And then, sure as shit, I see some red bouncing at the ditch culvert. Running dark, but the trailer brake lights still on the circuit. My experience last time tells me that Pete and I aren't ready for the Randolph Scott sort of deal—riding and shooting—if shooting starts. I need to be on foot, but close enough before I dismount that I don't end up blowing like that bull they called Gordion Snot which I rode down in Albuquerque. But that's another story. My mind's wandering while I wait.

The pickup pulling a trailer comes to a stop almost opposite me, maybe a hundred yards but behind the haystack. Pete and I are still on the west side of the creek, opposite. This is even better than my plan, but I'll take credit for it. I'm thinking, if I were a rustler... those lights. But I guess whoever he is he's thinking he wants to be on the cable so his trailer brakes work. A little forethought and selective wiring would have taken care of keeping them dark. But I'm not him. Of course, with my own trailer, I can lose half a season trying to figure out why my lights aren't working right. That might have been the reason Pete and that Paso Fino stallion never got the job done. She probably cycled in and out, while I was looking for the loose wire. My mind's drifting again. Let me try to focus.

The truck on the other side of the haystack shuts down. I can hear some of the cows trotting down toward the stack, hooves on hard ground. They're expecting to be fed—it's off-schedule, but what the hell, to them it's hay. About ten minutes later, I hear the doors open and close behind the stacks of bales. Then three quick chirps from a silenced gun. I give the rustle-fellas time to get into their work, bleeding, hoisting, skinning, severing the head attached to the hide with a cordless sawzall; split the gut and let the entrails drop. I can visualize it as I sit on Pete who's a little anxious, but I pat her neck and she goes to dozing again. They're talking, low if at all, and I can't get a feel for it over the sound of the creek. Just a word here and there. Like pros they must know their work. You gotta admire anyone who's good at his profession. In an eight-to-four existence, what else is there in life but a little self-congratulation and a tipper-up for a job well done at the end of the shift?

There's ice on the edge of the creek, but it's flowing nice in the center. The chuckle and sigh of the water covers Pete's passage. I take her nice and slow. I dismount, tie her off with the Mc-Carty on a stackyard post on the backside of the stack, and pause to calm my breathing. I've been in big moments before. My first bull—or for that matter, my last one. Or... my first one-handed try at a brassiere hook. Focus, damnit! I remind myself again.

I see movement out of the corner of my eye. I turn my head, my hand on odd-number, but it's just a dog, which whines recognition and approaches. Holy shit! "Snickers," I whisper, squat, and pat her on the head. She licks my hand.

Once again, the unexpected. Now, what the fuck do I do? I take a tip from my new compadre, Dick McDougall. I'll let the egg pickle in the vinegar. I'm visualizing purple beet juice, and pepper-corns, a clove or two of garlic, and whatever else has sunk to the bottom of the jar. I got enough pockets in this jacket for a flask of Evan Williams. I wish I'd brought one with me.

It's What You Know

I wait until they're ready to leave. I hear Leonard's voice on the other side of the stack "Snickers!" He waits. "Damnit, Snickers!"

"Git," I hiss at her, give her a shove. She goes away like she's done something wrong. But she goes. I move around the corner of the stack as they leave. They're taking it real slow, driving by feel and memory. I know the contour of the trailer, I think—an aluminum Titan if I'm not mistaken. The gut piles are shiny in the dim starlight. I also know the route they'll probably take to get off of the hay meadow. I might get out ahead.

I lead Pete to an abandoned beaver cut tree by the creek, use it to mount, and cross back over to the other side. We hurry as best we can through the grove. I get down and open the gate, cross, close it, then hustle Pete to the trailer and load her.

I head in the direction of the old highway. Without slowing, from a half mile through the ditch-watered cottonwoods I can see, a couple of vehicles, parking lights. Transfer happening, I think. Or maybe something else. I cruise south on the old highway past the gravel pit, past the storage tanks for the propane company, a well-lit yard, locked. Everybody knows a propane thief respects a padlock and chain, and a terrorist can't climb a fence or carry fence pliers to nip the wires. Western ethics at work. Homegrown Homeland Security. There was an article, in the Gazette about that, about hiring a night watchman. But nothing ever came of it. That would have cost everyone a nickel more a gallon, so it's just as well. Still I can imagine the grant writers are busy, bless their satellite pop-up business plans.

I head south on the old highway picking up steam, around the curve, then slow down and pull onto Ellie Hysom's ranch road. Ellie doesn't come to the highway and into town unless her grandkids are playing soccer. The season is over. She doesn't maintain the road very well. I ease one set of wheels to the high center and one set in the dry thistles. I can get out of sight behind the hump where Ellie ransomed off a spot to the cellular company for a new satellite tower. By looking to the north, I can see the cut-over to the interstate, and in the other direction I can look south down a stretch of the old highway. I pull up the grade near the tower, shut down, chock one side wheel of my trailer with my favorite rock, unplug, unhook, crank down, pull forward, close my tailgate. Driving past the gas tanks earlier reminds me of two things. If I'm not back, I'll call Jensen in the morning and ask him to come over unsaddle Pete and haul her to some water. The second thing I'm reminded of is that I need to pay my propane bill.

But, shit, this is more fun than kick-the-can! It'd be perfect if I could celebrate with a congratulatory punch under the ribs with some 86 proof. I want to succeed at this game, but I've got to start thinking ahead a little more.

Pretty soon here comes a Ford Powerstroke diesel with the trailer. Sure enough, a Titan. No way he can see me below the tower, against the light coming up in the east unless he's looking pretty hard. The Powerstroke rolls on south. I'd hoped it would cut over to the Interstate. Following him on the old highway would tip him off. As soon as he's around the curve, over the river, and through the woods on his way to grandmother's house, I turn myself back to the highway, take the cutover, and get on the interstate. I can beat him to the next off ramp at Middle Fork. I'll cross under and park like I took a break as I head north on the off ramp. If he doesn't come east to the Interstate on Middle Fork Road, he's going to be driving by a lot of ranch houses and end up at the intersection in Kaycee. I'm guessing he'd rather not, wherever he's going.

I am over on the side, just far enough up the ramp I can see down Middle Fork Road, looking west. I watch with a couple of hills between the old highway and the four lane. Don't you know it? Not five minutes and Smokey is behind me with clack from his siren and flashing lights.

I kinda know the guy in this district. Don't know his name, but... "What's up?" I ask as he walks over to my window and taps. I lower it.

"Troubles?"

"Nope," I say. "Just tuckered out. Needed to take a break." For once I'm glad I'm not drinking.

He does the computer thing on my plates, asks for registration, insurance. I present them in return for a warning—not having current stickers on my license plates. I showed him they were still stapled to my registration.

"I'd say you'd better get those on before you get back on the highway," he said. "Something you should have done last February. You gotta display 'em to be in compliance."

"Yes sir. I appreciate the reminder. And I'm a complier—mom always said... ."

He looks at me for a moment, sensing, I guess, that I'm a smartass. But he lets that go. "Have a nice day. Oh, and the scenic pullout isn't that far. Safer than taking a nap on the ramp. Don't forget to buckle up." He walks back to his car.

While this is going on the Powerstroke and Titan have come and taken the ramp south onto the Interstate. I can guarantee two things: he doesn't like to see Smokey, whichever way he's headed, and he won't be speeding. Easy does it. If I hadn't been otherwise engaged, I might have tried to share a little chat with Smokey, just for a chuckle, to show him there were no hard feelings. But he's probably in a hurry too. The first batch of donuts may be out of the fat and being sugared somewhere down in Casper. He backs down the ramp, crosses under the interstate and heads south.

I get out with my flashlight, and act as if I'm wiping the dust from the corner of each plate with my sleeve before putting on the stickers in case Smokey might still be watching. I stepped back to enact some admiration for the tag job, just to complete the panto-mime.

But Powerstroke is out ahead. I'm guessing he won't be pulling off at Kaycee to visit. Over the next rise, I get the taillights of the Titan in sight just after the South Fork of the Powder River. I stay back. This is one of the things we learned at Drummond. Information. "It ain't who you know, it's what you know," the retired cop at the seminar explained, trying to be funny, "The difference between a private detective and a snitch—well there is no difference, but what a P. I. knows keeps him out of jail and pays his rent. Sometimes both."

This past night has informed me, unless I'm dumber than I think I am, that Leonard is rustling his own cattle with some help, or, I suspect, up until recently, having someone rustle them for him, while he played the game of being a victim. And what I want to know is where are these three carcasses going? To complete the trifecta I want to know who's driving that Powerstroke Diesel. I'll start with that short list. Too much wanting to know can overload the circuits.

Who You Know

I keep my distance, thinking about things to stay alert. Lester Woods comes to mind again. A ramshackle ranch close enough to Canada that he could adopt a hockey team. Why did Flegel keep in touch with this odd duck? Of course, they were both in country at the same time, at the same base. But Vietnam, by my estimation, is something most folks have forgotten. Those who haven't wish they could—but when they can't, well, that would be Lester Woods. And why would Leonard go so far out of his way to drop Snickers for breeding? If I was a Dashiell Hammett detective I'd have me some answers for the next chapter, but I've lost track of chapters and I'm just playing this detective game by the seat of my pants.

The sun's up when we get to Casper—me with Powerstroke ahead. I coast down the off ramp and wait until he's turned right, then I go left—a little more deception, but I got him in my rearview mirror. I take two quick lefts and I'm on a street parallel to the main drag south, hanging back. I am not entirely guessing when I go around, look down an alley, slip by on a side street and see Powerstroke with Titan backing up to the outside dock of Conchita's meat department behind the supermarket. Grass fed beef, I'm thinking. Popular choice. I get out my binoculars. Juan and another aproned fellow help roll the carcasses in on an overhead rail. Up before sunrise and call ahead for curbside service, I'm thinking. They were waiting for him.

I go out around my pickup as if inspecting my box in the back to give a look at the driver, but the suns up, and I'm looking straight into it. What I can see mostly is the dust on my binoculars. Still, I get a glimpse as the crew passes into the shadow of the doorway. The guy driving the Powerstroke is nobody I know—short, saggy jeans, Teddy Roosevelt moustache, high-crowned brown hat. The license plate is from South Dakota—I write down the number.

Okay, so I'm through for the morning. Again, following the advice of my newly adopted mentor, Sheriff McDougall, I am letting the egg pickle. I go find something to eat at the same place I ate the last time I was down here around breakfast time —the joint I promised never to return to. Everyone deserves a second chance to do a bad job. That's been my fortune in life. Still, in its favor, this greasy spoon's easy to pull into on the way out of town. And to my satisfaction, the biscuits and gravy, early and fresh, aren't that bad.

Wish I had a sidekick, for consultation. I've got some information itching to be shared. I now know something that I didn't know, under my hatband. Maybe a call to John Woo.

After gassing up north of Casper, and against my will, pissing in a stinking urinal, while reading the delights associated with the Thrilla in Chinchilla (a condom with a fake collar of fur) and Cum Clean—"...she'll confess she loves only you...," available for eight quarters from the dispenser above the sink, I head north with a container of coffee in my caddy hole. I am beat, but I make it to that pullout next to the elk fence at Tripple T. I've used it before—an overflowing garbage dumpster, paper drifted into the fence wire, makes me feel right at home. I snatch some zees, idling, heat on, window cracked, but for less than an hour. Naps sitting up give me major aches.

I get out and stretch. The chill air reminds me to call Jensen. Jensen says he'll borrow his boss' pickup that has a hitch and go get my horse trailer and Pete, haul the works over to the propane yard and water up my mare there. I ask him to unsaddle her first, tell him I'll be by in a couple of hours—and thanks!

Then I punch up John Woo's number. I get past the reassuring recordings about how important I am. I enter Woo's extension. I'll be goddamned; he picks up..., again!

"John Woo," he says in a tone of voice that is all professional.

"Hey, John. This is Gabe Brindle."

"Gabe, how have you been?"

"Good, good." I hate this greeting bullshit. He doesn't care how I've been or he would've called to ask. And, in the last couple of days I've found out that someone used my own gun to kill my dog, and that the guy who hired me to protect his herd from rustlers is now rustling in his own herd.

I'm not sure how much I should tell Woo, but I kind of fill him in, then ask, "I can make an arrest, right?" I have doubt all over that. "I mean, I'm within my rights, right?" Too many 'rights.'

"If you're suggesting a citizen's arrest, that's very iffy. It may be time to transition your information to law enforcement." Gee, that sounds familiar. Has my lawyer been listening in on Drummond? I hesitate.

"That's my advice as your lawyer. But, why?"

I roll out the whole situation for him. But who the heck am I kidding. I won't arrest anybody. Wouldn't if I thought I could get away with it.

"I think I left my coffee by the printer, honey. Would you bring it to me?" I gather he's not talking to me. But then he is. "It's an insurance scam."

"You think?"

"Insuring your husband up to the hilt, bumping him off, or an empty motel, victim of an unexplained fire. Buying futures in the stock market and then betting against yourself, a little three card monte, or follow the pea in the shell game."

"Flegel was divorced," I say.

"Oh, I'm not talking about your client's dead ex-wife, I'm just saying that amateurs want to get into the money too, but not everybody has a hedge fund for a sandbox. Your average avaricious amateur finds marriage handy and tempting. But, I've never heard of a rancher stealing from himself."

And I remember Mother Brindle again: "It takes money to

make money.”

"And, I imagine he's getting a cut on the grass fed beef that's going across the counter in Casper. He'll get paid for it twice."

"Sweet, huh?"

"You got pictures, I guess."

"No." Well, so much for my new mail order digital camera. I forgot about it. I hope he can't feel the heat of my ears burning. "Nope. But I got the license plate on the trailer."

"Criminals are known to commit crimes, but not often in their own vehicles."

I feel stupid enough to go back to driving water truck out in the gas patch.

"But all is not lost," he says. "I've been meaning to call you."

"About what?"

"Let's follow up on the self-rustling rancher before I get into my good news."

"Okay."

"Just in case anyone has spotted you poking around, lay low for a few days. Then go to the sheriff. He, or the insurance company—probably both—are going to want a deposition from you. I'll be there if you think you need me. In matters such as that we bill by the hour."

Another reason to try to wrangle a final paycheck out of Leonard, I'm thinking, while he self-rustles.

"But the good news—"

"Lay it on me."

"I was back to a law class reunion—not an anniversary, that's for old guys, you know." He titters. "One of my classmates, well—I won't get into the backstory—he's running for prosecutor down in Weld County, Colorado."

"Good for him.," I say, hoping he can hear the yawn in my voice.

"The guy's going all the way to the edge on crime fighting, an Old Testament conservative campaign. Stand your ground with a vengeance, eye for an eye, tooth for a… well, you get the picture. He figures there are enough old school nut jobs out there in the Colorado farmlands that he can get elected. A lot of people are pissed about the marijuana thing, you know. They're still raising wheat, corn, and soybeans. They're old school. And if they've been quietly raising pot on a spare acre or two, the price was much better when it was illegal. Still, bar fights, DTs and DUIs are good enough for most of them." He snickers. "They want a way to fight back, kick butt—druggies, illegals, gays, an uppity Black man in the Whitehouse. He's going to run on a batch of issues—red meat for everyone, all in the name of law and order."

"Gee, that's tremendous news, John," I coo. "Is he looking for an endorsement from a range detective?"

"You're not serious, are you?" he asks.

"All is definitely not lost on you, John."

He sighs for the purpose of my hearing it. "Do you know the Krauss family?"

"Drank a few Krauss ales, but I just couldn't develop a taste for gelding piss."

"Well, according to my ex-classmate, they're hiding behind and filling up the bucket for Citizens United, deep cover, them and the Freaumonts. They're putting their fingers on the scale of a lot of local campaigns."

"Who's Freaumont?"

"Owns the semi-pro soccer team, but old money from somewhere. Nobody knows, or if they do, nobody's telling."

"Which citizens are these, specifically, that got united in a togetherness sort of way?"

"Long story."

"Give me the Readers Digest version, then."

"The point is…."

"What is the point?"

"My classmate from college, well he's dating the daughter of the cousin of the appointments secretary of Krauss Brewery fortune trust—something like that. Being a private detective, you probably get it that everybody knows some little tidbit about something else, or someone else. To most it's just a game."

"Fine. but I don't know what that has to do with my little bubbling pot of rustling information."

"It doesn't."

"Well?"

"The parole board at CSP."

"I don't get it."

"My classmate owes me a favor the nature of which I won't discuss—but it will pay dividends until I say 'stop'."

"That's swell," I say.

"So, his would-be fiancé is in the Krauss orbit. And, I'm only asking for a tickle in the right spot."

"I still don't get it."

"Trust me."

"Well sure, not a problem. I mean, who ya gonna trust?" I was going to go all the way to Ghostbusters, but John's on my side, I think.

"A little note in each folder of the parole board participants when they convene next. They like to be remembered for their civic duty. And the warden—well who the hell would want that job? But most of them do, so...."

"What does the note say? 'For a good time, call Isaiah Brindle, cell number....'"

"No. Just a tug on the chain from the warden who serves at the pleasure...."

"Who's pleasure?"

"I have no idea. I'm just new at B. R. O., remember. But Mother Woo explained to me how things work."

"How's that?"

"Well, things are connected in amazing ways."

"That's amazing," I say, and add, "Pardon me while I stretch—I've run out of yawns."

"C'mon, Gabe. Water runs downhill," says Woo.

"That's even more amazing."

"Let's wait and see. Your brother might be home with some new jewelry before Valentine's day."

"You're serious?" I ask. "You want to call in the favor your classmate owes you to get my brother sprung?"

"Oh, don't worry. Not a favor. But ethical considerations don't allow me to call it what it is. The easiest way not to say 'no' is to say 'yes'. A small return inside the brotherhood of thieves—just joking. Pure as the driven snow. As I say, 'It's the gift that keeps on giving.'" Annoying giggle. "Like my professor in evidence class used to say: In trial it's what you know; in life it's who you know."

"This is good news, John," I say. "Does this classmate of yours believe all that shit he's going to campaign on?"

"Not a word of it. But he's a born politician, and you have to start somewhere. So, he's starting with the rural reactionaries in Weld County, Colorado. He moved to Greeley a couple of years ago, so he's almost a local."

"He must owe you a helluva favor."

"He doesn't owe me a darned thing, except rent on what he wants me to keep forgetting. I'm just a storage unit." Another snicker. "Pictures too. A fraternity party, and I brought the video camera."

"I thought better of you, counsellor," I counsel.

"College pranks," he says.

"No. I mean about belonging to a fraternity."

"I didn't. It was his idea. I was his guest. But enough about that."

"You can't get into trouble, can you?"

"Everything is deniable, and he'll never try to pull the plug. It's a nearly painless way to demonstrate that, 'We're all in this to-gether.'"

"You're pretty free in sharing information that you didn't want to share."

"If you become the source of a leak, I'll call you a liar. Who are they going to believe?"

He has a friendly but low opinion of me. Join the club. But I'm still curious. "So, this friend of yours, down in Weld County...."

"I didn't say I had a friend in Weld County. I said 'if I had a friend in Weld County.'"

"I thought you said...."

"It was a hypothetical. Must be a bad connection."

"So speak louder. But should I try to talk to Ike—hypotheti-cally speaking?"

"Well, there's always a chance the candidate in Weld Coun-ty will stall, but not likely. It's election time, so everybody's got an angle, cleaning up, suppressing evidence, making new friends, reassuring old ones, petty extortion known as politicking—democ-racy reborn. But let's just wait until Ike calls you for a ride...if he calls you for a ride." A pause, then, "And you may want to renew our relationship."

"I don't contribute to political campaigns. I want nothing to do with the Weld County candidate"

"Did I say there was a candidate in Weld County? I said, 'If there was a candidate—"

"Your classmate," I interrupt.

"I don't know what you're talking about. I always skipped class."

"Oh, you want me to help pay the rent on the plastic plants. Why didn't you say so. I didn't know it had lapsed."

"Like an insurance policy," he says. "Pay and pray." A sniggle.

"You unscrupulous Oriental," I say, and immediately wish I hadn't offended him with my best Warner Oland.

"The practice of law can get very boring. But we're all sworn officers of the court, so we do nothing unscrupulous while the end justifies the means," he laughs again to negate what he just said. "Still, fun is fun, like the firm's family picnic day. A kegger with sack races, horseshoe tournament—you get the idea of the firm's usual definition of fun. So, I appreciate our relationship."

"Well thanks," I say.

"Keep me posted but stay out of trouble."

"I will."

"Thank you, honey."

Again, I gather that he's not talking to me.

"Gabe, they're waiting for me."

"Yeah, okay," I say and sign off with: "I see the UPS truck outside. Gotta go." But he's already hung up.

Priorities

Too much to think about. Woo told me too much. I'm over-loaded. Time to go through the prioritizing process again. That's the difference between bull riding and my current job. Bull riding, I had eight seconds, to find out whether habit, instinct, memory, and guts were going to get me to the next go-round. And even though the bull might have wanted to kill me, he didn't hold a grudge, and his motives were usually clear. Well, except for Son of Slam who was an own son of Slamma Jamma. I believe he inherited a grudge from his grand-pop, Uncle Slam, who was said to have a corkscrew for a soul—if bulls have souls. The rodeo stock company that bred that line of bruisers still makes a contribution to the PRCA schol-arship fund in the name of any cowboy whose career he claims was cut short by any of their stock. Focus, I encourage myself.

Okay, first thing is to go past the propane tanks and pick up Pete. Next, drop her off at Tortilla Flats and then go visit Leonard— just a friendly call, and to ask for an advance on my next month's detective work and to get the news if he's cooked up any. I could just have him send the advance to John Woo, but we all get a tick-le when we're allowed to hold some fold for a tick or two. Then, stop by McDougall's office to accept the offer to become part of the sheriff's re-election team. That should put me well into the after-noon, and after a nap, time for a philosophical pick-me-up snifter, a chuck wagon meal, an after-dinner beverage, and another nap leading to retirement for the night.

Take care of the horse that brings you home, I repeat what my friend down on Blue Creek used to say. So, I go after Pete and my trailer.

At the dealership tanks I see my mare tied to a post, but I don't see my trailer. Jensen is hanging outside in his coat, doing maintenance on his delivery truck. The urgency of hunting season is past. He leveraged his week off at the end of the rut, got his elk.

"Boss's hitch wouldn't fit yours, so I used his trailer. And your trailer is still up by Hysom's road. Your saddle's in the shed."

"Hey, I appreciate your help," I say. "I'll go get my trailer and come right back."

"Why don't I just trailer your horse down there. I can use the boss's truck. He don't care."

So, I load Pete in his boss' trailer, throw my tack in the back of my pickup, and he follows me down to Hysom's road. As I couple up my trailer, and plug in, he says: "Gabe, not bugging you, you know, but I'm still hanging fire for your propane bill, you know, the delivery, you know, so I could go hunting, you know."

"It's on my list," I say. "Tell your boss or the person who does the billing that I have never stiffed anyone on a debt, however I've been on assignment and I haven't had time to sign the checks my bookkeeper has written and left on my desk."

"Well, yeah," he smiles. "Why are you parked down here on Hysom's hill?"

"Watch for it in the Gazette," I say, hand on door handle.
But Jensen wants to talk. "Leonard Flegel's got him a new tractor."

"Thought he had a new tractor," I say.

"A newer new one," he says. "An 8R. It's too pretty to use. So, he'll probably just have to leave it set in the yard, or build a shed to keep it out of the weather…"

"Thanks for taking care of Pete."

"A lot of tractor," he says, walking alongside my open window.

"Yeah."

"You, can't beat a Deere."

"See you, Jensen. Thanks again."

"I always wanted me a Deere." He trots alongside. "But the family farm went belly-up, and…."

"Gotta go," I say.

"Want me to bring you an elk steak?" he shouts as I get ahead of him and begin rolling up my window.

I stop. Roll the window back down. "You can eat elk?"

"You know you can, Brin. You're always kiddin'."

"I'll give it a try," I say. "But, I gotta go. Thanks for your help, Jensen."

As I reach the old highway I see him in my rearview, turning his boss' pickup and trailer around. I'll have to compensate for my rudeness over a beer when I get a chance. Every Mike Hammer needs a friend who's reliable and doesn't want to know too much.

Pete's glad to be home. Hay to soak up some of the water Jensen offered her. Then I turn around and head to Flegel's. When I pull under the interstate, I can see the new tractor next to Leonard's truck. I was never a tractor man. I admire it nevertheless, as I pull up. Anything shiny will get me to turn my head. Flegel's probably watching.

I go to his back door and knock. Snickers is by the back steps. She yips once, sees me, and relaxes.

From inside, "Come in."

I pat Snickers as I enter, "New rig in the driveway."

"Yep. Methane wells. I can hear the environmentalists yapping all the way to the bank. But the bad news.…"

"I know what you mean. I've always felt that way about a new tractor."

"Nah. They're at it again."

"They?"

"Whoever. I went down to throw out some hay—it's about that time of year, starting the daily grind of feeding—and I found three gut piles."

"Be goddamned!" I hiss. Appropriate dismayed shake of the head. "What the hell is going on?"

"Well, if you'd do your job, maybe we could catch them."

"Don't start in with me, Leonard," I say. "It's a cat and

mouse game. And the cat will eventually win. Be patient. And I have a fill-up of propane I need to pay for. So, if you can manage to advance me enough to keep the bill collector away, I'd appreciate it."

"Goddamn, Brin. I'm paying a helluva lot for no results."

"That's the thing about results. You can't rush them. But the next time I'm ready to go out, saddle up and come with me."

"Gave up the horses; they went through the sale barn. You know that," he said. "Kinda hard to do a sneak up on a rustler with an ATV. But Jesus, Brin, can't we catch these people? They're gonna hit the road and all I'll have to show for my effort is what I've paid you."

Nicely acted. I go along with it. "You see, Len. A criminal gets the idea he can risk one more go-round, just like a bull rider. He never gets out of the game while the gettin's good. So, I say, we just pretend nothing happened. Don't bellyache at the sale barn. Don't moan at the Co-op. Everything is great as far as you're concerned. Get it? Meanwhile you and me need to sit down and polish up the new plan I've been working on. One that's bound to work. I reserved a role for you—you'll fit right into it."

"Sounds like a bad idea already," he says. "If it's like the last one. But you won't make a move without me, right?"

"As I said, there'll be something for you to do. When the posse rides, you'll be there. Remember who I'm working for, Len. And while we're on that subject, I'm serious about my propane bill... and I need a little to cover operating expenses."

"A month ain't passed since the last time."

"No, but I'm planning ahead. And us range detectives work by the week. So, I want to keep my calendar clear. After all, I'm dedicating a piece of my future to you."

"Well..."

"I don't know your business, Len, but with a few methane

wells, you're bound to have a bulge in the petty cash fund—I mean, don't you?"

"Conchita wants a new pickup."

"Everybody wants something," I mumble while trying to get my mind to process how a Deere, 8R, would be a useful vehicle to deflect attention from the movement of money. But I've been watching too much TV. Still, I have to get my ideas from someplace. "If we don't catch the bastards, I'll give my fee back. Besides, you got a new Deere."

He looks at me a little defensively. "Like I say, methane is just another cow belch to me, but the company with the lease has a half dozen producing wells. You're sure you're working on a plan?"

"I got a hunch. And I've read a couple of novels where someone has a hunch that really pays off—at nearly the end of the novel. They made a movie out of one of them."

"We're not in the movies, Brin. This is reality."

"Goddamn, I hope so!"

"So, tell me about it."

"Well, you know how reality is—hard to pin down."

"No, I mean your plan. We have to get a move on. My herd insurance company is getting itchy. They're wanting to know. I told them I had a detective working on it, and he didn't like being interfered with."

"You didn't!" I saw trouble coming. "And there ain't nothing like a visit from an insurance adjustor to screw up a plan."

"They said they'd get to my problem as soon as they can."

"And?"

"They're lying."

"How do you figure?"

"They're probably on their way already. But they don't want me to accidently tip their hand for them. They want the rustlers to pay another visit. Then they come in all gangbusters and snatch 'em in the act."

"You're pretty suspicious, Len."

"But, I bought you a little more time. I told them you were ready to turn the case, and all your evidence, over to the sheriff." He smiled.

"Well, that fits right into my plan, and into South Dakota," I say with a wink. "That's where your answer lies."

Leonard turns to give me a hard stare, then breaks into a laugh. "That's why you want gas money?"

"South Dakota's a big state."

"So I hear. How much?"

"Fifteen hundred—not to mention the propane fill-up; but if I have to drive over five hundred miles, I'd like mileage too.

"What are you planning on doing in South Dakota?"

"That's what I'm going to find out. Not to mention that when I'm through with South Dakota, North Dakota's next. But I'll stay in touch."

"Okay, I'll write a check."

"I don't like checks."

"You don't trust me?"

"I don't trust the IRS."

"I'll bring the cash by your place later. When you leaving?"

"As soon as the weather breaks."

"Weather's fine."

"Oh. Right."

On the way back into town I explain to myself that Flegel wants me seeking, but not finding. What better place than the Dakotas? I'm just part of his scam, part of the picture, a board certified dummy to keep his insurance company happy. Regardless of the license plates of that pickup backed up to the dock in Casper, I bet nothing is going to South Dakota—just like John Woo said. But Leonard will be satisfied if he thinks I'm off on my way to a wild goose chase.

I find Sheriff McDougall heavily into crime solving and domestic tranquility with his feet up on his desk, eyes closed. He tips his hat back, then lays it on his desk. "Gabe," he greets.

"Sheriff," I begin.

"Call, me Dick, like I said." His friendliness is back.

"Dick, I think I'd like to join your re-election committee."

"Well, good. Part of the unpaid staff."

"I wouldn't have it any other way. Democracy lives in the good hearts of volunteers."

"Say, you have a way of turning out a saying. Could I borrow that one for the after-election shindig? That is, if I win."

"Be my guest. You know as well as I do, that when you pay somebody you get the idea that the good ship, Loyalty, is floatin' on greenbacks. But that's not how I operate, Dick."

I'm itching to tell him what I've learned, but privacy isn't part of a sheriff's office. Neither is confidentiality. All the little watching and listening gadgets that Homeland Security grants have bought. Rumor down at Welles' Pit has it that over in Washakie the lady working the desk found out that the deputy in charge of building maintenance was watching on a mini-cam when she pulled down her skivvies in the restroom. They didn't fire the deputy, they fired her for not being a team player. She's got a lawsuit going. The deputy called in sick; a few days later he showed up to work with a swollen eye and a broken jaw wired together. He claimed he had gotten cross-wise with an angry cow he was helping calve out. A late fall calving heifer? That's the story I overheard down at Welles' Pit. They got it from someone coming over the hill that he had to suck his oatmeal and raisins through a straw after it was run through a blender. Well, I'm not a gambling man, but I'd bet on the woman's husband. And that's another thing. If I am going to continue doing the Mike Hammer on horseback, I gotta get hold of some of that electronic stuff that can watch while I'm off doing something else. Maybe the sheriff and I can come to an understanding.

He gets back on the phone to clarify his pizza topping for the lunch that his newest deputy, Reliance Nygaard, is picking up. While I wait some more, the idea of a Wyoming Small Business Grant pops into my head. I read about it in the paper. I'll have to go to that seminar, if they have one. There's always dung beetles hanging around bullshit. One of them might help write a grant application for me.

Promoting plans seems to be in the air.

"So, are you going to buy coffee, or not, while we discuss your plan?" asks McDougall, standing up and putting his silver belly back on his head. He leads me out the door.

"Didn't you just order pizza?"

"A cup of coffee is just code. Like in baseball when they say a player is invited up to a major league team for a try out. He don't even unpack his bag. He just has a cup of coffee. In other words, don't take long. My pizza might get cold."

I turn down a ride in his car. It's probably wired six different ways. I suggest my pickup. He agrees. Re-election time and he's watching the budget. He gives me a good lawman's stare. "Like I said before. It's the last word in an argument..."

But I slip past his theme and give him a second appetizer. "What does a fellow get for stealing from himself?" I ask.

"Who's stealing from himself?"

"Same guy who has a new John Deere."

"Who's got a new John Deere?"

"Same guy who is diddling the brand inspector."

"Norma and him?" says McDougall. "How's he stealing from himself. To hear it from him he ain't got two dimes to rub together."

"He doesn't?"

"You're saying that he has a John Deere?"

"Who's that?"

"You mean someone else besides Raymond is bedding Norma?"

"Raymond's doing Norma?" I ask.

"You see her truck down at the barn all the time late at night. Even when the Smith brothers aren't shipping."

"There's a lot going on in this small town."

"Raymond has the run of the place, using the couch in the owner's office after dark."

Sounds to me like Dick's been watching. "Something new every day, huh?" I say.

"Oh, this has been going on a while, ever since she stopped buying tires from Bobby out at M B T."

"Was he selling bad tires?"

"Besides that."

"What?"

"He got religion."

"There was an outbreak of that some time back," I say.

"He confessed to his wife, and she went glory hallelujah all over him with a broom. Penitence is an ugly thing."

"An affair with Norma seems to be a dangerous idea. But she quit him," I conclude.

"Only after a couple of the tires he sold her blew. Then she did."

"But she was having an affair with Bobby?"

"She's married to Bobby. Still is, as far as I know."

"Norma?"

"No! Bobby's wife, Elaine. The tires that blew were on Norma's pickup. Factory seconds, no warranty."

Mountain Battery and Tire—I remind myself never to shop there. I gather Norma was getting a discount there for barter. And she got what she paid for. All news to me.

"But since when does Raymond own a John Deere."

"Not Raymond, Dick. Leonard Flegel." I turn and shoot a smile at the sheriff.

"Well, everybody knows that."

We ride. Sharing news with him is a disappointment. I hope he will come to some insight about what I might know so that I can confirm or deny. "Leonard's been rustling his own cattle," he says.

"Is there rustling going on in this county?" I say with a poor version of mock horror.

The sheriff turns, looks at me for a long beat—that lawman's stare. "How long have you known?" Then he turns back to staring out the windshield. "Why would he hire you to catch the rustlers if he was doing the rustling, you ask?"

"I didn't. But you sure know a lot," I say.

"I keep my nose to the ground. Just like Liggy."

"But where'd you get the idea I'm working for Leonard?"

"When you're in law enforcement business, it's good to know what you know."

"Who told you?"

"I'm not at liberty to divulge, but if you suspected that Norma told me, I wouldn't confirm or deny it."

We ride on. Eventually he gets around to asking for the details of how I know what I know. I give him a summary, not including the little ride to Casper to find out where the carcasses were going.

And I get around to asking him where I might expect to find a crew to put up his final round of yard signs. "Don't worry," he says. "My son has a number of deadbeat friends. I'll have him call you. Welcome to the team."

And then he backs up his thoughts for a moment. "Let me ask you something."

"Okay."

"You play checkers?"

"Never did."

"In checkers, the guy who makes the first move should always win. He has the initiative. So how can he lose if he knows what he's doing, and why play the game?"

I've always felt that way ever since I turned down my first checker game. Philosophy time. "Truth be told, Dick. I figure a checker player is looking for art. Setting things up. Playing them out. Seeing who gets to be the sucker."

He turns to look at me, and I don't want to meet his eyes. I squint out the windshield.

"Again, welcome to the re-election team," he says. "I got a feeling about this election. A landslide in the making, if we can make it happen."

That rings with a double meaning. And McDougall is right, it comes in a flash. Flegel thinks I'm an incompetent, a Drummond mail-order detective. Like I've considered before, I'm just for show. I damn near killed Maisley Martin by accident who's probably just another stiff with a larceny itch, and expendable like me. I shouldn't have told Leonard that I didn't fancy killing a man over a few ribby steers. That's why he wanted to keep me on the string. Came a time the act needed closing down, but he couldn't tell me to quit. For actually doing the job he'd hired me to do, he sent, or had someone send, a message to back off by killing poor old Finagler—a fake. And my dear old dog, the victim. But Flegel needs me for the show until he doesn't.

I'm back to my mantra, deep in my throat like a growl. "Somebody's gonna die for Finagler!"

"What's that tune you're humming?" asks MacDougall.

"Nothing, just clearing my throat."

"Sounds like you got something stuck. Might want to get Doc Rangel to look at it. Turn this rig around. My pizza's getting cold."

The Gotcha Question

We drive in silence.

I hate it that McDougall might think I was just being used for Flegel's scheme—actually, I hate to think that myself. But nothing like a little shop-talk to disrupt whatever we're thinking.

"So, you got the Sandra Johnson's murderer in jail yet?" I ask.

"It's comin'," he says. He's in a mentoring mood. "In my pie shop whoever's closest to the pastry is the Jack Horner."

"I'm not sure I get it."

"Or at least knows who the Jack Horner is."

I still don't get it.

"You see, on a pre-meditated murder—or even unpremeditated, or anywhere in between, like semi-premiditated—you got a corpse problem to think about. You can dump it, bury it, tie some cement blocks to it and take it out to the lake. Or, you can make it work for you. The mob likes to leave bodies around, lets people know who's in charge, what to worry about, who's next."

For a moment I'm thinking Finagler again—and, of course, the mantra buzzing in the background. But the sheriff continues. "In Ms. Sandra Johnson's case we got to figure out why her body was dropped off on Flegel's kitchen floor. But, for my money, Flegel's the Jack Horner. He's closest to the pie."

"Hell, he was married to her, Dick."

"As you well know."

"But you don't think Flegel did it?"

"Hell no. But he could have, now that you got Flegel doing his own rustling and stiffing the insurance company, I bet a little talk-see, about all that's goin' on around the county could prove interesting... if the time comes and I find the time."

My first thought was that I hope the sheriff is lazy enough to put it off until tomorrow. Len might forget to bring me my money if he gets all jammed up in contradictions.

"But, no hurry," McDougall says. "Eggs are in the vinegar. Let 'em pickle. Timing is everything just before the elections."

While Leonard visits my bungalow on ball bearings to drop off the money, I get a call from the sheriff's son, Dick Jr., who says he's got a couple of friends aching to do some yard invasion. He's all in, he says. I figure that's the only way he'll get his allowance. So, we set up a time and place to meet later that night. He'll bring the yard signs.

"What the heck were you talking about on the phone there?" Leonard asks. "Signs and all that?"

"The Ouija board. Got me an expert to interpret the signs."

"Seen that on TV. A movie. I didn't know people actually did it."

"Only as needed," I say. "When the spirits are on the move."

"You believe in that stuff?"

"Heck no. It's just a game. Same as that fellow they got down off the hill that is occupying a bunk in the sheriff's office annex. Lie detector test or Ouija board—same thing. But the onliest thing I truly believe in for crime solving is what you dropped by. And I appreciate it."

Leonard takes off. I have a snifter and a short nap, then wake up with an uncontrollable urge to reward myself with a home cooked meal. No one should ever deny that sort of urge. I go to the cupboard to discover that I have only a can of chicken noodle soup. Perfect. I give it a little warming on the stove, find some saltines which are distinctly stale and sit down to a meal only a negligent mother would serve and congratulate herself.

Then I drive into town to meet up with Dick Jr. and his hoodlum friends. The sheriff was right. The crew wouldn't know which way was down if it wasn't pointed out to them. With me giving directions, we get rid of about four dozen of the yard signs which say: "DON'T sell yourself SHORT on law enforcement. Re-elect Sheriff

McDougall." We plant them beside any sign we see promoting Phil Short's candidacy, and where the lights in the front room aren't still on. Of course, some yard lights on motion sensors come on, but we hit and git. As the sheriff explained, people get accustomed to signs during election season. By the time they figure out they've got an extra one the polls will be closed. The last six signs we plant in a row on the courthouse lawn. It's after midnight, but I buy the boys a couple of six packs at the back door of Fort Liquors, which, of course, is scrupulous about not selling carry out after midnight, and drop the boys off at Dick Jr.'s car. I'm all tuckered out.

Then home. I find my butcher paper with the circled names and lines drawn between, give it a study while nursing a liberal double. That shiny new Deere and the salesman from Billings are missing from this diagram. I write him in—Norton Weems, his name known to me from my involvement in Flegel's divorce—testifying, that is. Then I draw a line to Len, and a line to Sandra Johnson's corpse. What does that explain? It would work on TV, an insight after a commercial break, but it means nothing to me.

It seems like the gears in my brain are stuck, so I have another dose of rust-buster. Sure enough. It is revealed to me—I'd like to say in a flash, but it is more like a light slowly coming on—that if I knew what Weems might know, I might truly make my bones as a private detective. I determine to make a trip to Billings, but the drive is just under three hours, and I don't intend to make it just to find out that Weems is off peddling jolly green giants in the wheat lands of eastern Montana at pre-holiday mark-ups. After waking late, dosing with aspirin, I call the tractor dealership.

"Is Norton Weems in?" I ask the woman's voice that answers.

"I'm sorry," she says, but she doesn't sound like she is. "He's over in Miles City."

"When will he be back?"

"Tomorrow, all day. Whom may I say called?"

"Frank Peete," I improvise. "An old college friend."

"I don't think Mr. Weems went to college," she says.

"Yeah, me neither," I say. "Joke, you know."

The silence suggests she's shaking her head... or rolling her eyes. "I'll leave a note that you called, Mr. Pete."

"That's Peete, with two e's after the p," I say. "And one after the t." If I'm going to use an alias, I'd like it to be spelled correctly.

"Yes sir," she says.

The next morning I start pretty early. I try to work out a plan in my head about how I'm going to be cagey, ask Weems the "gotcha" question, and get a telling answer. I've found that most plans aren't worth a shit, though—at least if they're mine. One of the last plans I made was how I was going to ride Dipsy Doodle. Brilliant! After that I promised just to climb on and get the smell of the bull and take it as it comes. Dipsy dumped me like a load of guts when we were hardly clear of the chute, almost stepped on me, and then trotted back to the pen. Roger Crane, the smart-ass bastard, said, "You could've just scratched and saved yourself the trouble of getting on him, as short a time as you spent up there." But I got even with Roger by screwing his honey in the back seat of his own crew cab where she invited me. He'd pissed her off about something. "Gabe," she had approached me. "Can you do me a favor?" I did. Always lend a helping hand. It's the code of the West.

Funny how when you're drifting back on a recollection the road can just slip by. I wonder if that's what old folks do rocking on the front porch, reliving the old times, getting to do it all over again, two for the price of one. The next thing I know I'm at the connection to I-94. But I continue on with 90 and get off and backtrack on the frontage road to a yard full of green tractors.

I go into the building that has the maintenance area in the

back. I figure I'll find Weems up front, not with a greasy rag in the shop. There's a counter behind which a receptionist looks up with the silent question of raised eyebrows. "Norton Weems?" I ask.

There's an office with a glass divider behind her. I can see Weems through the transparent wall, sitting at his desk. I recognize him even though he looks different with his pants on.

"I'll see if he's in," she says, and picks up the phone. "And who are you?"

"Frank Peete," I say.

"Oh yes, Mr. Peete. College days," she gives me a wink.

Now she thinks it's funny...I'm funny.

"Mr. Peete to see you," she says after punching a key. To me she says, "You can go back." She points to a hallway.

I'm thinking that this is a lot of formality to talk to a tractor salesman that I spied on but who never returned the favor. When I walk in, he gets up from his desk and only then recognizes me. "What're you doing here?"

"No way to greet an old friend," I say.

"What do you want?"

"I was thinking about an A-9 tractor," I say.

"You make that much money lookin' through keyholes?"

"Well, that's the whole thing about it."

"What?"

"I'm about ready to lose a paying client. When Leonard Flegel gets arrested he's bound to want to talk about his new tractor, and your old flame."

"Let's go out and look at some equipment," he says loudly. He slaps his Resistol beaver on his head and grabs his jacket.

We exit out back to the lot of used farm trade-ins.

"I ought to kick your ass, Brindle," he starts out his sales pitch.

"Not saying that you shouldn't, or that you couldn't," I say. "Just betting that you won't, and that you wouldn't want to be the first guy since Hopkinson to be executed in the state of Wyoming."

"You're full of shit."

"Interstate extradition takes a little longer, but they'll be coming for you." Boy, I'm on a roll. I feel like a magic hand has scripted this. It recites like a true crime novel.

"You playing cop, now?" he asks.

"Nope, just serving my client. He's paying me good money. It's the least I can do."

"That fucking Sandra Johnson," he says, almost to himself. "Nothing but trouble."

"Well, her troubles are over."

"That's what I heard."

"But are yours?" I rub my lower lip, Bogart-like.

"A more scheming person…."

"I used to know a judge that told me, 'Dreams and schemes can get you twenty to life'." I was almost on the last page of the script.

"Swell. But he wasn't talking about Norton Weems." He gestures himself with his thumb.

"Well, far be it from me to be the bearer of bad news."
He ignores me.

"She wanted his ranch, and I was supposed to be the gofer. But she didn't know shit about cab-over tractors. I couldn't even get her to buy a riding lawnmower."

Nice diversion, but that's not the subject.

He puts his hand on the fender of a backhoe. "She never gave up on trying, and she was a woman for a grudge."

"Is that why she never took off her glasses?"

"Fuck you. And fuck Len, too, except he likes John Deeres."

"Don't talk bad about Len. He ain't the nicest guy, but someone has to pay for taking pictures."

"You know what they say about thieves…."

"Like?"

"They're partners until one figures out how to steal from the other."

"Well, I guess you know your thieves alright."

"You figured out yet that Flegel's stealin' his own cattle?" he asks.

"I'm shocked at the suggestion," I say, calling on Claude Rains again.

"It was Sandra Johnson's idea. And that Mexican dame down in Casper, fronts the beef in her meat department."

"You gotta be kidding," I say, jaw dropped for emphasis. "But, how would you know about that?" I smile, still it seems everybody has known for a long time what I found out the day before yesterday. It doesn't seem prudent for Weems to be talking about it so openly—except that he assumes, dogged detective that I am, that I already know. But if he only knew how little I know he'd snap his yap. They talked about the burden of knowledge at the Drummond seminar. "It isn't what you know, and it isn't who you know," said the retired cop. "It's knowing when to act like you don't know anything—and keeping your mouth shut." That's hard for me to do, but I compensate for it by saying stupid things.

Back to Weems, I say, "That's part of the reason I'm here. My trick knee tells me that this leads directly to Len's new tractor."

"The pitiful bastard."

"Down in Rawlins I hear they put a new paint job on the death chamber and they're itching to drop the handle on the serum. That'll be the end of shiny green toys."

"You're full of shit, you know that? No way I killed her."

"Then why did Flegel get a new tractor? Apparently, he's got the leverage—or you do, or somebody."

"Good trade-in value on the old one. Hardly used."

"Correct me if I'm not getting it, but Sandra Johnson told him something about you and that's been his leverage."

"Aside from size of my appetite and my bad taste in women, she didn't know anything about me."

"Well, I hope you screwed better than what I watched. Now, I'm guessing again—you may not know a thing. But…." I pause for effect. "The sheriff down in Muddy Creek County is holding Maisley Martin…."

"Tell me something I don't know," says Weems. "I know Martin. We've done some business. He finds me customers. Is that a crime."

"I'm not a cop. I don't know a crime from a pile of shit. Not my job."

"Then why don't you just stop wasting my time—unless you've changed your mind and need a tractor." He turns to go back toward his office, expecting, I guess, for me to follow.

"Question," I say to his back. He pauses, doesn't turn. "All in all, you weren't bad—you know on the DVDs. And the divorce lawyers amused themselves with them for a while. But given that gadget you were working with, did Sandra Johnson ever have an orgasm?"

He spins and rushes me. He's slower than a bull which is a good thing. I sidestep and kick a leg. He goes down, his head taking on the wheel rim of the backhoe.

I return to the building. I hand one of my cards to the receptionist. "Have Weems call me if he wants to make the trade."

"What? He didn't come in with you?"

"He got busy checking out the wheel on a backhoe and forgot completely about me. I'm in no hurry, but I'm kinda in a hurry, so, see you."

She gave me a toodle-do with her fingers, looked at my card. "I thought your name was Peete?" Then she answered the ringing phone.

On the way south I stop for gas at some pumps and a convenience store on the edge of Billings. I pick up some pork skins, an Almond Joy, and a large coffee. It's mid-afternoon, and looks like it wants to snow, but probably not. I find a radio station broadcasting the second half of the Carroll College, Dickinson State football game. Last contest of the season the announcer reminds us. The Carroll season hasn't been a roaring success, but the coach wants the team to go out on a positive note, and so on. I don't know anything about either of the colleges, except Carroll is Catholic, but it beats listening to canned oldies or a preachy station. I decide to be a fan for the Catholics whose team is called the Fighting Saints. It doesn't hurt to be on the side of a gang which has God and the Pope in the locker room for a halftime peptalk. Before I drive out of range of the radio station, the Saints are losing by two touchdowns. I'm not superstitious but everything I touch.... And on the other hand, it really isn't everything.

I don't know what I've accomplished by this trip, but I stir up McDougall's pickled egg analogy for extra meaning—and that doesn't get me much either as the peppercorns settle. Still, for sure, Weems is tangled up in all of this. To use another of the sheriff's analogies: he's close enough to the pie to be a Jack Horner. I decide I need to find out what the term "analogy" actually means. I've used words often enough for the wrong purposes or in confusion that it'd be good to try to follow Miss Mason's admonishment. "Gabriel, before you use a word it's good to know what it signifies, where it came from, where it's going." I got a dictionary back in the trailer somewhere.

I drive on. That pit stomach feeling, like I used to get when I was little and Mom was going to find out. Ike and I could hear her getting out the belt. Still, nobody is going to give me a whipping, I hope.

The rush I got from confronting Weems has evaporated. I realize I'm sad and a little afraid. Even shouting my mantra at the windshield to remind me of what I owe to make it right for Finagler only gets me feeling better for a little while. My eyes fill with tears. I hear myself saying lowly, as if there were someone in the cab who might hear, "I wish I had a friend."

"There, there, good buddy," the passenger in my mind answers back. "Wax your gear, and on to the next arena."

I pull out on the Lodge Grass exit and dial up Frankie. "What're you and Chris and me having for supper?" I ask.

"Hadn't made any plans yet," she says. "But I didn't plan on cooking for three."

"Well, that's the plus side of planning. Now you can."

"Truth is, Gabe. Tonight's not a good night to invite yourself over. Chris and I need the evening alone."

"Oh, I won't be any trouble," I say. "And, if you're having a little lover's quarrel, maybe I can referee."

Silence at the other end.

"Well, we're still friends, right?"

"Friends forever, Gabe. But friends know how to hear 'no.'"

"Well, I heard that. Still, I also thought I heard you double-clutching so you could change gears. But it might have been my front wheel bearings."

"Not tonight, Gabe." Firm.

"Talk to you down the road, Frankie."

"Sorry, Gabe." She hangs up.

Ain't nothing to loneliness, I think, that Evan Williams won't make feel better... until tomorrow. I hurry up and get on home.

The Scale Of Our Crime

While I'm feeding Pete I give her a little philosophical chat, something to think about because I'm still in that mood. "We're on the short list," I say as I consider her eyes. "Names get called off the list without warning. Time's up! That's all she wrote." Pete nuzzles down into the hay I spread, looking for the alfalfa leaf. "But the executioner says, 'Before I give the signal to the firing squad, any last words?'" I watch Pete chew, the ripples of her jaw muscles in the yard light. "What would you say?" Pete doesn't say anything, of course. "I'll expect a little more from you in the morning after a night to think it over," I say and flip the snow from her forelock.

It might get serious about this first snow, large flakes in the wind, temperature dropping for sure. I enter by the back door of the trailer—the only door. Inside I turn up the thermostat on the space heater and listen to the burner pop on.

You can say this about loyalty. If someone is always there when you're needy, never says no, just asks, "How can I help?" And will climb into bed with you and not crowd you too close, that would have been Finagler. Tonight, though, it's gonna be the bottle. "Thanks for the offer," I say giving it a wink.

I turn on the TV, find another ballgame. It's being played someplace where they're still picking oranges and worrying about dehydration from sweating. The broadcasters are discussing time-outs, clock management, and lost opportunities. I've forgotten to go to the store for supplies. I do have some cereal, but no milk—I threw that out, rotten, a few days ago. In the good old days milk use to sour and curdle. Don't get me started.... So, I skip the meal and go directly to the after-dinner snifter. Before the ball game is over, I kick off my boots and take to the couch.

Banging on the door brings me back to reality. My mouth is dry, tastes awful. I lift my H & R .44 off the peg and shout. "Whataya want."

No answer.

I stand over to the side, my practiced routine. "Listen up. I got an AK-47 pointed at the door. Whataya want?"

"Brindle?" A voice I should know.

"Whataya want?"

"It's Norma."

I open the door. "What the hell, Norma. Why are you visiting dysfunction junction at this time of night?" Actually, why is she visiting at all?

"Can I come in?"

"Well, shit. Why not." I look past her. That snowstorm has arrived.

She steps through the door, looks around. I can almost hear her asking if I ever clean the place. And I can almost hear myself saying, go to hell, Norma. An example of a conversation better left unspoken.

I throw a pair of soiled jeans off a chair onto the bed. "Shake off some flakes and have a seat" I say. "What's so important that you're out in a snowstorm? But I wish I'd known you were coming. I'd a had you bring in some carry out."

"What's Leonard told you?"

"About what?"

"You know, everything."

"Oh, that."

She looks worried.

"Well, he's told me just about everything, or a little less— I'm not sure. But you can fill in what's missing."

"Have you talked to McDougall?"

"About?"

"You know."

"Well…."

"I had nothing to do with that."

"What'd I just say?"

"So, who do you think did it?"

"Did what?"

"It."

"Oh, that. Well, that's not my job, Norma."

"So, you haven't talked to McDougall, right?"

"Look, Norma, I'm getting confused. Are we still talking about that, or something else?"

She looks around my trailer as if there were someone listening from under the soiled clothes. She mouths a word.

"I didn't get what you said, Norma."

"The rustling," she rasps a whisper.

"What a man does with his own cattle is his own business."

"And the other stuff... I told him I'd help until he had made his deductible."

"How's that going?"

"Oh, he's way past that. But he wants to keep at it. That's going to look funny to the insurance company—everybody loses a cow now and then, but he's losing a lot of them. And, he's got a detective working on it, and a policy."

I assume she's referring to me. "Well, nobody ever accused me of being good at this detective stuff. I just make a show of it." I gather Flegel told her what I was up to. "And nobody ever accused Len of being a good judge of character."

"You know the insurance company's going to send somebody. I signed off on the losses—I can do that, you know. Verify them, just like with predation, vehicular....."

"Yeah," I interrupt. "So, time to stop. Get back to horses out of the corral, the sale barn, ..., and Raymond."

She cuts her eyes at me. "Who told you that?"

"Small town, word gets around."

"Sandra Johnson," she stumbles on what she wants to say. "You would think, wouldn't you?"

"Well, if I was thinking I suppose I would. Just speaking

friend to friend. But I'm off duty."

"We're not friends," she says. "Not really."

"Care for a beer?"

She shakes her head.

"Do you mind …?" I go to the fridge and take one of the last two.

"What happens, say…," she starts again. "If you know a crime's been done, and…, you don't tell the authorities."

"Obstruction, or accessory—something like that," I say. "After the fact. Or before. Or somewhere in between, depending on whether it's just carelessness or on purpose. That sort of thing." I surprise myself sometimes that I've read the stuff Drummond sent to me, and actually remember some of it. "I'm not sure, one or the other—give or take a fact or two." You hear it in television shows.

"And Leonard," she says. "That's all he seems to want to talk about, his former wife. How she didn't make him feel... well you know."

I don't, but I say, "Oh that." I go for broke. "Did he kill her?"

"Now that's not a very intelligent question." She smiles just enough. "Would he kill her out somewhere and drop her off in his own kitchen?"

"Well, he's alibied. But you know?" I take a thoughtful draw on my beer.

"Len don't have the nerve anymore to kill somebody. According to what he told me, never really did, but…."

I shift the tack a little. "Dick's got some opposition in the election. That murder gets solved and he's a shoo-in."

"Dick, huh?" she says. "First names, now?"

"Well, it's election time. Everybody is everybody's friend."

"Then let me tell you something. I don't give a good god-damn about that lazy turd." She's narrowed her eyes and is coming on with an attitude. "I could care less if he gets re-elected. But I need out of this whole thing. Rustling, a dead woman, and Leonard's new tractor, that disabled vet up toward Lodgegrass...."

"Getting complicated," I agree. "But what disabled vet?"

"Leonard said he sent you up there after Snickers."

"He told you that?"

"Yep."

"He's not as good at keeping secrets as you are. But why do you think he sent me, and paid me for the trip? Cheapskate that he is."

"He wanted to send me. But I met that man once. I said, 'no way!' He's crazy. He hasn't got over Vietnam. But, back to me. I'm getting out of this whole mess. I should never have got into it to begin with. I'm going off to Utah where my sister is pretending to be a Mormon."

"So, you came by late at night in a snowstorm to share that news?"

"And, you know they're bound to be on their way."

"Santa's reindeer? Who're you talking about?"

"The adjustors from the insurance company. Isn't that what they call them—the investigators?"

"Well, yeah. If you don't have an investigator, you hardly got a crime. And rustling on your scale of crime, that's when you're really into deep water. A dead body in Leonard's kitchen is nothing compared to claims against herd insurance. Insurance companies will cover a massacre as long as you don't make your deductible."

She looks at me. I'm not sure she agrees. "Where'd you hear that?"

"I read it in a crime novel—no, it was on TV. But on the other subject, Norton Weems killed her," I venture.

"Nope, but I bet he knows who did. And about the horse-meat."

"The horsemeat?" The guessing game has outlasted my beer. I toss the can toward my trash can and go to the fridge for the last one standing. Norma doesn't know what she's talking about.

Weems has the most to lose, and I'll bet Sandra had him by the short hairs. Besides, the only way Flegel goes cowboying is in his pickup or on an ATV. Horses are gone.

"Well, there's nothing more to say," she says.

I try a fatherly summation—a voiceover from some B movie. "So, Norma, you are burdened by what you know, and by your involvement. You are seeking a clear conscience, but failing that you're looking for a way to escape the dragnet that is being deployed, as we speak, which will snare the great and the small from the…" I lose my train of thought, then continue. "However, never asleep, the watchful eyes of law enforcement scan the western landscape…"

"What the fuck are you talking about, Brindle. Sometimes you don't make any sense at all. Like I said, I don't give a damn about the sheriff's re-election. But I want you to talk to him for me. Set it up. Tell him I'll fill in the whole story with a promise from the county attorney that I'm not going to jail. Then I'll pack up and head to Utah. If he says 'no deal' then we never had this conversation."

"You want to cop a plea—to put it in the most legalistic way?"

She removes the plug of tobacco from her shirt pocket, bites off a corner, rolls it in the saliva in her mouth, and clamps down. "I guess, if that's what you call it," she says through her teeth. She gets up and goes to the door, spits off to the side. Standing in the door she asks, "Will you do that for me?"

"Why don't you just go to Dick yourself."

"I don't trust him. I won't talk to the Sheriff unless I have a deal."

"Well, a friend in need…."

"And Gabe, sorry about your dog getting shot while you were out of town."

"Yeah, he was a pal. I miss him."

She leaves. I go to close the door, and notice the snow has stopped, but the wind is pushing the stuff around. What the fuck? How did she know about Finagler? "Norma!" I shout to her as she opens her truck's door.

She turns. "What?"

"Come back here." I'm standing in my stocking feet in the snow on my back step.

But she gets in her pickup and pulls away.

Needs Assessment Plans

I crush my beer can and balance it on top of the trash by the sink. The world can get ahead of you, I say to myself. Too many details to keep track of. I need to go down to Louise's Laundromat with a couple of bags of laundry. I need to pick up the garbage in the trailer and take it to the barrels out by the barn, but they're full; so I need to make a trip to the dump. Gourmet dining needs constant attention and my microwaveable cache of food is depleted. Mental note, I've been yearning for some Spagetteos. And on top of it all, I have to try to finesse McDougall with Norma's offer so that he owes me. Mother Brindle used to say: "If someone owes you, you got your finger hooked in his belt." But if Norma killed Finagler—my mantra tries to resurface. Or maybe she just heard about the lowdown deed: the sheriff told her—but she's not talking to the sheriff. At least she says she's not.

Might be just about time to transition the great rustling conspiracy over to the law enforcement, I say to myself. Nothing that can't wait until tomorrow, though.

I toss the dirty clothes off the bed and get under the blanket. I wake myself up with the usual complaint and use the toilet. A new day can deceive you into being carelessly optimistic. I still have some coffee so I get that going and then to the shower. After a cup I feel like I could take on the world. I uncover the two duffle bags that I used to carry some of my rodeo gear in, load them up with dirty clothes, groan under the counter for a box of Tide. I put that all in the back of the truck on top of a layer of snow. I pull around to my barrels, load them, tarp, and bungee them, and wonder what happened to the good old days when you could drive trash uncovered to the landfill, and on a windy day leave half in the barrow pit, and that way save money when crossing the scales. That's another thing to lament about the passing of the old West. Then I'm off to town. On the way, I have my cell phone plugged into the cigarette lighter.

Norma Smith is a pain in the ass, for sure. But if she knew my investigating the rustling going on in Flegel's field was just a red herring to satisfy due diligence for the insurance company, why would she kill my dog, which she accidentally as much as admitted last night—or at least she'd heard about it. When your guilt gets to working on you, things can slip out. But here's the trouble. I almost plugged Len, after applying the bright light of my logic, cause and effect, and the rest of that bullshit to the subject. And my mantra was working. With Norma, at least, I had as close to a confession as I was going to get. But another home invasion wasn't on my to-do list. Particularly since I didn't know exactly where she lived: but I did know she was the baby sister of two brothers and they inhabited a cluster of houses resembling a compound out on lower Nine Mile. Which helps me moderate my plans to "vengeance is a good thing only if you have a good chance of living to enjoy your success." I try to pump up my mantra, but it doesn't help much. And I really wonder if Norma would do such a thing.

I go directly to Louise's and find enough empty washers not out of order, divide up my clothes, dump in detergent, and run a ten-dollar bill through the change machine. There was never a Louise at the laundromat, I'm told. She was the late mother of the two bachelor brothers. She died before they opened the place so they named it after her. But Liz is there, hard of hearing, as always, just short of panhandling. She's not an employee, just hangs around being helpful, and picks up tips. It's a place to stay warm, and Liz is honest. She's a semi lip-reader if the shouting isn't loud enough. She knows everyone local who comes and goes. Takes interest in tourists—who tip better—to offset the transients who don't.

I get the washers going.

"Why don't you sort your clothes?" she demands loudly. "Keep your whites and colors separate."

"I'm not Better Homes and Gardens type, Liz."

"What?"

"I'm not Better Homes and Gardens," I yell at her.

"You got that right. It's too late to put in a garden. But spring will come."

I hand her the rest of my quarters and shout, "Give 'em a dry for me, will ya?" And, I'm off to Welles' Pit for breakfast. Sitting pretty. Most of the day still left and my laundry's underway. Shit, I can handle this. I'll go shopping, swing by for my laundry, a little parking lot transitioning with McDougall, stop by the landfill on the way home. If that doesn't sound like a plan, then I'm not Ma Brindle's oldest boy.

While I'm having ham and eggs, the ambulance goes north on Main, lights and siren. Ambulances always sound so goddamned important. The hangers on at the Pit speculate about which one of the gals whose getting-ready-baby-shower was photographed for the Gazette had an emergency while getting ready to calve. Off to the supermarket, then to the liquor store to top off the food pyramid, back to Louise's Laundromat. Liz has me dry and folded. Stuffed in my duffel bags. But she's pissed.

"Asshole," she says.

"Hold it, Liz," I say. "No way to talk to a friend."

"What?"

"Don't call me an asshole!"

"Not you. Some turd from Montana, using our equipment to scrub his floormats."

I like her proprietary attitude. Loudly, "Well, you know those Montanans. Not civilized like us."

"Tossed his jacket in with them. I told him he should sort. He told me to go fuck myself. What am I, a nun?"

"I gather he didn't tip," I say.

"What?"

"Did he tip?"

She studies my lips. "The asshole," she says.

I leave her a little extra for saving Wyoming's reputation, and load up.

Back to the sheriff's office. It's a little buzzy when I come in, receptionist and deputy moving faster than the normal glacial crime-solving speed.

"The sheriff in?" I ask.

Enid walks past me, "Nope. Out in the field."

"When's he comin' back?"

"Hard to say," she says.

The deputy on duty, baby-face Reliance Nygaard, looks up to catch my eye like I owe him some money or something. I do owe him, once, after he returned from a two-year mission to the heathens, he drove me home when I was so drunk I couldn't put my key in the ignition. He was a rookie then, and "Serve and Protect" wasn't just a slogan. Then he had to ruin the whole thing by trying to explain to me about some guy named Joseph Smith who had a pal, Moroni. Even drunk it didn't make any sense to me, so I don't remember the rest. And when I asked him if they were being held for trial, he gave up.

"Well, tell Dick I dropped by. I'll call later."

I don't notice that he's behind me, but Reliance follows me to my pickup. "You didn't hear?" he says.

I'm always jumpy when I don't realize someone's on my blind side. Happened with a bull once. I jerk a turn. "Goddamnit, 'Liance! What?"

"Norma Smith's pickup was found in the ditch out on county road."

"Well, it's slick in spots. She okay?"

"Pressley Parson though she had some bad luck. You remember when her tires blew that time."

"Yes, but maybe I've forgotten."

"Well, they did, so Pressley figured.... But somebody ran her off the road and shot her in the face. Must have happened last night. This morning Pressley was on his way in when he seen her in the ditch, thought she might need a tug up on to the road, or something."

"Jeezus Christ, 'Liance!" I say. "Dead?"

"Yeah. But you shouldn't take the name of the Lord...." His eyes... worried, I guess, that the lightning might ricochet.

"Oh, I wasn't," I reassure Nygaard. "Just hoping her soul, you know, makes it to heaven...or wherever."

"Okay, then. And don't say I told you, but I know you're on sheriff's re-election committee." He hurries back inside.

I shake my head. How's that news going work with my mantra? That's hard. That's the real stuff. Not your rumor or a wild guess about something. I get in my truck, but I don't start it up. Mind's running. Somebody's playing with a big stick.

Once when I was still waxing my bull rig, there was a five-thousand dollar winner-take-all down in Norman. Due to some dumb luck I was tied with Carvalho Bilbao, one of them Brazilians. Flip of the coin, and if you could ride Tristan Salty (an own son of Salton Battery—the headliner of the Salton Rodeo Stock Company—and why I remember all this crap I don't know....), you carried off the whole shebang. Bilbao won the toss, and rode Tristan. That was bad enough. A second place purse wouldn't fill my gas tank. But later that summer Tristan stomped a kid from Chadron who recovered enough to ride a wheelchair and drool down his chin. I always thought that could have been me. As I say, I never got beyond Joyce Kilmer. But Norma being dead has the ring of poetic justice to it. Saves me the effort, but steals my pleasure should it ever have come to that—and probably keeps me out of jail. I don't know why she shot Finagler or for that matter, if she really did. Too late to ask now.

Then I move over real quick to what should be concerning me. She came by my place last night, then ends up in the ditch dead. Who the fuck? But if anyone saw her leaving my place last night, the old Jack Horner rule would be full throttle. My thoughts aren't coming in order. I finally pull out of the Justice Center's lot.

Despite my good looks and athletic figure—overlooking the fact that I'm fat, balding, and gimpy—I'm not a vain person. On the way home I get to thinking that whatever he figures out about Norma's murder, the sheriff is still on the re-election clock. I expect a visit from Dick—the man at work out in the field—pretending to be oblivious to the end of the election season, still not shunning someone from the Gazette tagging along to write the story. I'm sure there'll be someone. Somehow, they might end up at my place. So, cleaning up my trailer jumps toward the top of the to-do list. I got some skin in this game too—the intrepid private detective, acting undercover, risking life and limb, to put up yard signs, living frugally, modestly, his eyes set on distant goals....

Long ago one of my discoveries is that every task can be broken down into smaller sub-tasks which, when properly executed, complete the task. But they allow for a half-time pause to recharge and refresh before the push toward the finish—as if four seconds behind the hump can be interpreted as "So far, so good." It didn't work often on a bull.

The Drummond agency had a hand-out on prioritizing—trying to be cute, or current, by calling it: "Needs Assessment: Getting Your Ducks in a Row." Heck, I knew that. I unload my groceries into the freezer and the cupboard. Done. Prioritize my cleanup. Done. Kitchen sink first. But, before that, a word from our sponsors. I open a beer and turn on the T. V. Then, maybe something comestible/digestible to go with the beer. Too early for three courses, so I tear open a bag of corn chips. They're a little bland. I try a squeeze of nacho cheese on them, into the microwave.

Fox News is ranting as usual. How can a batch of people stay outraged all day, every day, unless they've been wired to a hot shot—that, or someone has threatened to take their meth away. But just like my standards for house cleaning, my standards for TV chatter company are also low. I go to the sink. I weasel my hand through the cold stale water and the dirty dishes, avoiding a couple of knives to find the basket that's full of slimy stuff, tip it out to drain. Drop it back in place, add a burp of dishwasher liquid, turn on the hot water. Pretty soon I got foam climbing out of the sink. The knives are still down there so reaching into it blind could be dangerous. Better wait for it to settle. I'm already getting that glow of satisfaction over a job well done, and I haven't even done it yet.

These late October, early November snowstorms are often feints, but it's starting again. And I get the urge for about the third time this morning to think things through. I turn TV off. The point of watching Fox is not to think.

Whoever coined that expression, "the down side," was probably a bull rider. The down side of my new friendship with Dicky McDougall—never mind acquaintances: Flegel and Norma and Conchita, and Maisley Martin whom I shot in the leg and is coolin' in a cell—is that when people start dying on their way home, it's a pretty clear signal that things are getting a little desperate. Who am I to ignore desperation?

I feel a touch of panic—or maybe it's just too much of the nacho cheese. I need to calm down. Whiskey to the rescue. While I work on that, I check my H & R, and my Smith and Wesson odd-number. I'd feel silly wearing my web belt in my own house, so I just leave the two handguns on the table.

Next thought. That son-of-a-bitch, Norton Weems—laundering money, I figure. And I figure more, or is it the whiskey talking? Leonard Flegel wasn't pimping his wife just to get a deal on a new John Deere. After all, Len contracted the haying on his place for shares—all he needed a tractor for was a winter feeding and drift busting. Any old International Harvester with a Farmhand™, or a front-end loader can get that job done. The new green meanies were fairy dust for Weems to sell, and for Flegel to admire. The money was in the beef. The problem for Flegel was greedy Sandra, so back a ways, I got hired to do the Peeping Tom act. Divorce is easy—but I guess getting rid of your ex isn't. Still, somebody got rid of her. Who knows maybe he just wanted out.

That's the trouble with stacking the deck. If it works one time, you try it again until you're either caught, or decide to leave the game. More links in the chain the harder it is to leave. It's simple to poach someone else's steer off a pasture and put it in your freezer—if you don't get caught you eat well. But when the inspector comes to the all-natural butcher shop in the supermarket in Casper, you'd better produce the appropriate paperwork. The violet stamp on the hanging carcass is the easy part. What the Department of Agriculture pays its field hands doesn't require them to be attentive, intelligent, or bribe-proof. That documentation series probably started with Norma. Who else farther along? I don't know. Not my job.

I think I'm pretty choosey about the company I get close to, and I don't want to join the dead people who are turning up. As was emphasized at the Drummond seminar, knowing when to transition a case into the official files of the law is the trick. But, by god, I've dumped most of this in Dicky's lap without getting anything in return. Still, I may have an ace in the hole.

Right now, my worry is Weems—probably the bastard that got fresh with Liz at the laundromat, and was cleaning up some splash back. He's come south, covering his trail. I wouldn't be surprised if he watched Norma pull into my plantation last night.

I adjust the lights in the trailer house. Doesn't seem like a good idea to be standing at the sink doing dishes opposite one of my windows. So, the dishes can wait. They're used to it. I move the table so if I sit behind it I'm pretty much out of view. But the truth is, one of the selling points of my house on wheels, my tepee to tow, when I bought it was that the natural light is admitted. So, I draw the curtains, for what good it will do.

I should probably warn Flegel about Weems on the prowl, if he doesn't know it already. But my duties as a detective are just about wrapped up, a decoy for the insurance company, and a sucker. First, I'll call McDougall, to tip him off to be looking out for Montana plates while he's out investigating Norma's murder. Oh sure, Montana's fifty miles away—that would be a rare sighting—wouldn't it? But that will give me a cover in case I shoot the John Deere salesman in my driveway. As I pick up my cell, it goes off in my hand. I jump like I've been shot, drop the phone, recover it. I don't recognize the number. "What?"

"Gabe, it's John Woo."

"John who?"

"John Woo, Gabe."

"Oh, that John Woo."

"Aren't you happy to hear from me?"

Yesterday's News

My legal team informs me that corruption is alive and well in Colorado, particularly if you can lean on a little inside action. The connection, tenuous though it may be, from John's former classmate, via someone who has a line to the Krauss family who is backing the classmate's campaign, which is appealing to the yahoos in Weld County produced a result. Ike is coming out of the Canyon. He'll have to wear an ankle bracelet for a year and then he's as good as a free man, except for not having the right to vote. But us Brindles never vote anyway—not out of a lack of patriotism, but it's the only way to avoid making the wrong choice.

"I was effective and to the point," Woo says modestly.

"Why didn't you tell me?"

"What if I had bombed? You and Isaac would have both been mad at me. But I was down in Colorado anyway taking a deposition on a personal injury suit."

"You dropped over to Canyon City? I thought Weld County was up in our direction.

"Well, my witness resides in Pueblo. And I shuffled things around so that I could be at the prison during parole hearings. I was in the hearing room, and just like magic I was asked if I wanted to speak. That's how things are hooked up, all the way back through some political ambitions to a fraternity party that got out of hand." He tittered in that annoying manner.

"So, it went well?" Not that I really care except that it worked, but you have to give a guy's ego some breathing room to inhale.

"You kidding me? Some guy got fried in the CF & I foundry. He's a ball of scar tissue who talks by computer voice generation. The steel company tried to settle a couple of times but I'm taking it to the brink."

"You're on a fuckin' roll," I say. "But aside from that—I meant at Ike's hearing, you did well. I can't thank you enough.

Should I go get him?"

"Paperwork will take a few weeks. But I painted up Fort Fletcher like it was a Boy Scout camp, and you, the mentoring older brother, former world class athlete, etc., etc. Didn't matter anyway. When the Krauss family tells its puppets to jump, it doesn't matter if they're in the shower—they jump. As mother Woo used to say, a carp is only slippery if your hands are wet."

I heard a diesel in my driveway. "John, I'm sorry. I got to go, but damn, that's good news. Again, thanks from both Ike and me." I hang up.

I'm not opening the fucking door, whoever's out there, till I call McDougall. I punch up his cell, a number I've had since we did the signs.

He answers. "Sheriff."

"Dick, this is Brindle," I say. "I don't know who just pulled up outside of my trailer, but there're things going on in this country, and...."

"Okay. So what?"

"I heard about Norma. We gotta talk."

"Well, everybody knows by now. Can't keep a secret in this country." There's a pause. "But settle down. It's me, right outside your back door. I got a passenger napping in the back. I'll leave the truck idling and we can talk, if you'll let me in."

"Well, Jesus Christ, Dick. Why didn't you say so?"

"I did the first chance I got, but with all your whining...."

"Alright, alright. I'll open the door." I clear the table of my guns. The H & R on the peg. I drop the S & W in the pocket of my jacket hanging on the chair back. I don't like to demonstrate my worry, which some might call cowardice, in too many ways. I turn the deadbolt and open the door.

"Evenin', Gabe," says the sheriff. He steps in, removes his hat and flicks off a few snowflakes. He looks around. "What's your table doing over there?"

"I've been cleaning house."

He looks around. "You've got a little way to go yet, huh?"

"Wanted to have it all spruced up."

"What for?"

"You got something against a clean house?"

"Can I sit down?"

"Suit yourself." I drag the other chair out. "Care for a beer?"

"I'm on duty, so I'll have to limit it to one…, or two. Depends."

I go to the fridge, pop a top.

"Election's next week," he says after taking a deep draw on his beer.

"Yep."

"Norma gettin' shot couldn't have come at a better time."

"Guess not." A strategic murder, that seemed a little cold. I wait for him to continue but he doesn't. "Better be on the lookout for Norton Weems," I say.

"Why?"

"He's up to more than selling tractors. That fucker probably followed me down after he got over his headache. You know what's going on by now, don't you?"

"I've heard you use the expression, 'Getting' your ducks in a row?'"

"I use it from time to time when I can't figure out what's going on, and how to sound intelligent while what's going on gets figured out," I say. "But I'm telling you. Weems is…."

"So, how much more do I need to know. My ducks are getting in a row, even while I'm enjoying this beer."

"Is this a variation on the eggs pickling in the vinegar," I ask.

The sheriff smiles. "You're a man with an imagination," he

says.

I smile too. "Duck eggs, I would imagine."

He nods in agreement.

"But I wonder if Flegel knows who he's dealing with?" I ask.

"I expect he does. I got Reliance waiting outside of the Elks Club where Flegel is playing cards. Don't want to go all Wyatt Earp on him by barging in, you know. Election time, and all. If he's losing it'll look like I rescued him from his IOUs. The Natrona County sheriff will wait till we're done up here, then Conchita and Juan and the crew will take up some space in the Natrona County jail while they clean off the fingerprinting ink and wait for the bail bondsman."

"Goddamnit, Dick. Weems is on the loose…."

"Well, if he is, he busted out of his cell in the Yellowstone County Detention Facility."

"What the hell is that."

"Jailhouse in Billings."

I'm starting to feel like yesterday's news.

He finishes his beer. "You know, people like that grass fed beef even if it's a little tough."

"So I hear. The closest I've got to grass fed recently is one of Jensen's elk steaks, but without Finagler I don't have any use for them."

"Finag who?"

"My dog who died."

"Sorry to hear that."

I thought he knew. I don't start in on that. Doesn't matter anymore.

The sheriff taps a fingernail on his empty beer can.

"Ready for another?" I ask.

"Department policy forbids it, so sure" he says.

I hand him a second can. He pops the top. "I like beer in bottles better, don't you?"

"This was on sale. Watching the budget," I said. "Election time, and all."

"Anyway, things are wrapping up almost on their own. And Maisley Martin has had a lot to tell. He's been so cooperative I've almost started to like the guy. Heck, we let him out of his cell to sweep up the office. Saves money. Like you say, election time. Voters like that. And Martin probably thinks he's safer living in the jailhouse."

"I suppose he told you who shot Finagler?"

"Finagler, your dog?"

"Like I said."

"I think Norma did it."

"I think you'd be wrong, though I don't know for a fact."

"Fine," I say. "She came into my trailer and used my own gun."

"You're whinin' again. And that would be a nice touch. You wouldn't know it, but she had a good imagination. Brand inspecting can do that to you. But I don't think Norma had dog killing in her." He tips up and drains half of his can of beer.

I go to the fridge.

"By the way," says the sheriff as I hand him another beer. "Len's ranch is split-estate. He has surface, but WyoServe has sub-surface leases. They're pumpin' away."

"Which means?"

"He's methane poor, not methane rich."

"Which means?

"Gabe, I don't want to..." he doesn't finish that sentence. "It means he gets surface damage abatement, so much per well head, so much per rod of road. With those methane company boys, you make your deal and live with it while you try to figure out how to kick yourself in your own ass."

Ninety-Seven Percent Lean

Dick McDougall likes to draw out a story. Fills up the time when he could be out investigating, crime-busting, or doing something else. That's what all those Wednesdays down at the sale barn are for. To restock his supply—and a little politicking.

Back at the crossbar motel, in order to complete his induction into the brotherhood of flippers, the sheriff said Maisley filled him in on the horses. What wasn't mixed in with the extra lean hamburger in Conchita's butcher shop got mid-nighted to Canada.

McDougall actually asks for pencil and paper to illustrate the rate of profit when lean loin from a $500 horse weighing twelve-hundred pounds on the hoof is added to burger from an eight-hundred pound steer which costs upward to $1,900.

"Before I knew anything about this, I was passing through down there in Casper. I'd heard about the place. A good old fashioned grocery store with a butcher shop that did things to order. Since I was out on the county's time, I wasn't in a hurry, so I stopped. I watched them grind me a couple a portions, dropping in the cubed meat. Then a regrind and you got your 97% lean. Best burger I ever ate. I almost hate to bust up that end of the ring. I could just stop with Flegel and his insurance scam. But it's election time."

"Weems killed Sandra Johnson," I say. "I'm glad they got him locked up."

"You might have been right if someone else hadn't beat him to it. You ever hear of a guy named Lester Woods?"

I'm a son of a bitch! I don't think I'm really very good at this transitioning thing. It doesn't help that I got little to offer, or I'm barking up the wrong tree. "Where'd you get that idea?" I ask. I can hear the whine returning to my voice.

"Maisley Martin is good for more than keeping the jailhouse clean."

"You believe Martin?"

"Well, I believe what he said Lester Woods told him. He was

on his way with some horseflesh, you know, hello, Canada. They shared a bottle. That vet ain't right in the head if what Martin told me is true. Gets to drinking and…."

"Well Vietnam screwed up a lot of folks' heads."

"I'm talking about him videotaping dogs fucking—hooked up and all. Wouldn't let Martin leave until he watched a show. It's one thing to shoot someone, but watching dogs screw. Now that's sick."

"Why didn't you tell me about it sooner."

"About videotapes of dogs? I didn't think you'd be interested."

"No, about Sandra Johnson."

"Oh that. Because it wasn't none of your business."

For some reason that reminds me of a bull I got on once. More than most bulls, he'd figured it out. The quicker he unloaded a rider, the sooner he'd go back to the pen and something to eat. Rest up, wait for the next show, and do it all over again. So, in the chute, he'd wait till you relaxed. When they opened the gate he'd pause a beat, then explode. That bull was named Slo-Jack. He was one of the many sons of Jack Hammer who was a grandson of the hall of fame bull, Jack D. Rip. Slo-Jack had only been ridden once during the season. I expected to be dumped in a hurry. But I made it to the buzzer. I got high fives from the rodeo clowns, attaboys from folks behind the chutes, Alie Dee smiled at me while she did a fifty second interview. The next night, things didn't go as well. Slick Trick from the Sam Slick Ranch, that everyone seemed to be able to ride, dumped me right outside the gate and I hit my head. I got nothing in that go-round, if you don't count the headache. That's how I am feeling right now. Like, take two aspirins and call me in the morning.

"Mind if I invite my friend in?" the sheriff asks, gesturing outside. "I got the heater going, but…."

"Go ahead," I sigh. I wonder who's riding along tonight. He opens my door and waves toward his truck. That's when I see another set of lights sweep my turn-around.

McDougall is standing in the doorway, arm up gesturing. He folds up mid-wave. When things happen that fast, it's like they're in slow motion. The sound of the gunshot finally arrives in my mind. McDougall lands half in, half out of my trailer. I hit the floor on my good hip and fumble the S & W out of my jacket pocket. The sheriff groans but doesn't move. And there's Woods. He hops up on my steps, gun in his left hand. He treads on the sheriff's belly. I shoot. He falls backward, firing into my ceiling. Nothing too dramatic, unless you take into account I also shit my pants.

Woods is half off my back steps in the snow, not moving, but oozing blood. I turn Dick over and drag him in. He's gut-shot and making a mess. I fumble for my cell and call 911—tell the night dispatcher I need an ambulance, and why. Dick stirs. I try to come up with a movie cliché of encouragement. The best I can do is: "Hang in there, Dick. Help is on the way." This would be a moment when I could light a cigarette and press it between his parched lips. But we're not in a foxhole and neither of us smokes.

It's funny how events arrive. This is a pretty abrupt and unexpected end to my first big case. I press some clean towels on the sheriff's bleeding belly. I feel his pulse. He has one. I glance out the door. Woods isn't moving. On one hand, Sheriff MacDougall solved the case I was working on. But I helped a little, I argue in my own favor, not to mention I'm pretty sure I'm pretty sure that I killed Woods, who I'm pretty sure was after me. The Sheriff just got in the way. There's a little drama there. Not your Dashiell Hammett, damn it, but this is reality, not Hollywood.

I prop up MacDougall's head on a pair of my clean jeans. I don't know why that's supposed to make him feel better. I clean myself up a little and open my new bottle of Evan Williams.

And then I hear multiple sirens.

Teamwork

Liz from the laundromat is waiting in the sheriff's cab. The sheriff was going to use her to ID the Montana truck. She slept through everything that happened. Later I find out that I hit Woods in the throat. That's a pretty small target. I got lucky, or he got unlucky. Win some, lose some, zero sum.

Sheriff McDougall enjoys his landslide victory from the hospital bed with tubes draining him. On election night he's past most of the pain, but on a drip—probably a little happy juice along with the electrolytes. So he's in a magnanimous mood—I can use that term; as anyone knows, it's often heard on the bull riding circuit. The Gazette reporter is in the room, the local radio station gave up fifteen minutes of satellite golden oldies in order to send an idle sportscaster to do an interview. Mrs. McDougall whom I've never met, a smaller version of the sheriff in a print dress, keeps dabbing the sweat from her husband's shiny face. He thanks his re-election team and the people from the county for their vote of confidence. Even Phil Short comes by and stumbles through his short concession speech from the sheriff's bedside. And something I didn't expect, the sheriff gives me credit—but, not for helping put out yard signs in the middle of the night, and not even so much for my shot which accidentally closed the files on Lester Woods, because the sheriff knows Lester was gunning for me and he just got in the line of fire.

"Gabe Brindle was part of my undercover outfit," says the sheriff re-elect. "He put his own life at risk." Then McDougall adds, "Democracy lives in the good hearts of volunteers." That sounds even better when he says it. He gives me a wink.

This is an "aw shucks" moment for me. But I rise to the occasion and utter something stupid concluding with: "It was a real privilege to be part of the McDougall team of law enforcement professionals." Then I was able to hand out six or eight of my Need to Know? Complete and Discrete. G. Brindle cards (phone number at the bottom) before I left.

Anyone who has an inkling of how money moves from place to place, and justice works, will not be surprised to hear that Leonard Flegel's tractor was put up for his bail until he could bargain a guilty plea, and then it was sold along with a portion of his herd in order to make restitution to the insurance company. He, Conchita, Juan, and Weems are all enjoying a vacation away from the hurry-scurry of life on the outside. They'll be out in a few years.

Maisley got off with time served and five years parole. The fellow in the brown high crown hat who pulled the Titan trailer to Casper with me following has never been found. The registration turns it up as rented from a fleet truck outfit in South Dakota.

John Woo was right. You don't drive your own rig on that sort of a law-breaking excursion. Len's ranch is being managed by his neighbor whom he never trusted. But who did Len ever trust? He'll be back to ranching in a few years if his neighbor doesn't figure out how to take his ranch, and folks will begin to forget, or all else failing, re-tell the story and smooth down the rough edges down at Welles' Pit.

I actually finish cleaning my trailer. And I promise myself I'll never let it get that messy again. Then I drive down to pick up Ike. He needs a place to bunk until he can find a job and his own place. So, he'll have the couch for a while.

Home Is Where The Heart Is

Except for Finagler, I try not to be a sucker for sentimentality—oh sure, there are endings, you know, of Casablanca, The Light That Failed, Shane, Old Yellow, Sounder to name a few. But as a nostalgic ex-bull rider I prefer Slim Pickens at the end of Dr. Strangelove. So, I should expect some dampness when those come around on the TV. But this isn't a BBC movie.

I try not to choke up when Ike steps out into the free world for the first time in nearly twenty years. I struggle for a moment and wonder where those years have gone. Willy Nelson should intrude with his version of "Ain't it Funny How Time Slips Away." But on the way down to Canyon City I put myself on a diet. Too much sentimentality can ruin the stew.

As we embrace, I can feel Ike's tautness, the result, I imagine of working out in his cell, and nervousness.

"Snap out of it, pal," says Ike after a deep breath.

"I'm just happy," I say after a double swallow.

"You're the older brother. Try to set the example the character witnesses at the hearing pinned on you." His cheeks are dry.

"There were character witnesses for me? Do you remember their names? No matter, you get what you pay for."

Ike doesn't smile. He's been practicing gritting his teeth way too long.

"Well, let's hit the road," I say. "But you're not allowed to drive."

"I'm on the GPS so we won't get lost," he says pointing to his ankle bracelet.

We get into my pickup. "I brought a bottle; we can taste a little to celebrate." I point to the bag on the floor of his side.

"I don't drink anymore," he says.

"Not that you had that many opportunities in the Canyon," I say. "Except for homebrew. Still, you can always pick up where you left off. Time's a-wasting."

He shakes his head. "You talk about opportunities," he says, looking straight ahead after snapping his seatbelt. "Moonshine has turned into a full-scale operation in that place. Pay at the commissary and the bottle of Pepto-Bismol comes with your food." Again, no smile.

"I know prison cooking's bad," I say. "It's supposed to be, isn't it?"

"You know it."

"Pepto-Bismol?"

"Some jet fuel they cook up in the shop."

"Good stuff?" I encourage.

"If you want to pickle your brain."

"So, you abstained."

"Made a decision to get over to the right side."

"No! You turned in your coveted Brindle credentials and went religious!"

"Brother, brother," Ike tried a single syllable laugh. "I'm still a Brindle. About the only thing I had in the joint was me. So early on I decided to take care of what I had. Nothing more to it than that."

I exhaled a sigh of relief. Ike was loosening up and we were barely to I-25.

"Well, that's all behind us now," I say hopefully. "The future is straight ahead—and maybe off to the side a little, but still ahead."

Ike shrugs. Pause. "Did I say thank you?"

"Not in so many words," I say, trying not to sound hurt.

"Thank you, brother," he says.

Again, I have to give the moment an extra blink or two. We are headed north.

"So, what you been up to recently?" he asks. "You told me when you'd stopped bullin', then stopped driving water truck, then quit ranching. I figured you might have married a rich widow, but all of them with eyes and teeth that bad have been snapped up, according to what I hear." His Brindle sense of humor is trying to bubble up.

I fill him in on my new career, and without going into details on my early apprenticeship as a peeping tom, I tell him of my recent success.

Around Torrington we get quiet and thoughtful again. I ask him if he wants me to turn on the radio.

"Nope," he says. "No end to noise in prison. Everything hard and clanging, echoing; everyone shouting. People never shut up and stirs mostly talk to remind themselves we're all still alive. Even in ad/seg."

We ride the rest of the way saying hardly a word; get fuel, make a piss stop, and a coffee recharge.

What's Next

One thing is clear; life is not a detective novel. Nothing's worked out in advance. Who would have guessed that Ike and I would be sheltering in my trailer. It's hardly big enough for me and my mess. This is not a permanent solution, I hope. He's doing his share—things I neglect and preparing our meals. Nothing fancy, but better than Spaghettios—actually home cooked, sorta. Keeps a neat fridge. Doesn't rag on me too often for my bad habits, but I can see it coming. I'm already on rations as far as Evan Williams goes. And a six pack of beer can last days. He cleaned the barn and found my horse medicine there too.

I don't get to play the TV much. It disturbs his reading. He's learning to use my computer which I've seldom used after I completed my course with Drummond. I've had it since the folks at Sky-O-My started selling satellite service. They put the dish on the barn. It works most of the time. I drive Ike to the library once a week. This reading thing could get out of hand. Where would the world be, I shudder to think, if that habit made a comeback?

I also drive Ike to the meetings with his parole officer who is somebody I knew from Welles' Pit, but I thought the fellow was just missing social skills. Ike's got him chasing after permission for him to work at the sale barn.

I am able to negotiate with John Woo with the promise of doing a complete and discrete job for him now and then. We'll keep in touch. And he might pay a little better than I'm used to.

On some weeks I get a call from a potential client. I pick and choose. I tried using the parking lot up at Walmart in Sheridan for client meetings. Dumb move. Almost everybody I know in Fort Fletcher hauls their money out of town once a week to keep the sweat shops in Asia or south of the border humming.

Down at Welles' Pit people don't move away from me as quickly as they used to. But eventually. And that's no place to meet a client anyway. So, my office hours are held wherever I park my truck and take a short walk.

They say there's a period of time when a snake that's shed its skin has limited sight. Well, that would be me. But I'm seeing a little clearer now. I get a kidding type of elbow in the ribs from Frankie when I get invited to join her and Chris for a birthday, or some other excuse to celebrate. Friends are few and far between and that makes me appreciate her all the more. She's taken to calling me Longwire. I pretend I don't know who she's talkin' about.

That fictional sheriff in those Craig Justin novels has a drinking problem, I recall. Well, that's where the similarity between the two of us ends. You see, my drinking is both a pleasure and medicinal, but not a problem. But for a while I've got to put up with my brother's Carrie Nation urges. Maybe I'll buy another one of those novels someday, or check one out at the library, and see how he's handling his alcohol consumption.

From time to time, I think if my life were totally a fiction instead of just an occasional lie, it could have turned out a lot different. Which demonstrates a good use for falsehoods. They can keep you on the straight and narrow when reality throws you a curve. Don't get me wrong, I'm not opposed to reality in principle, but a little bit of it can go a long way. And I like to pick and choose when I can—a mixture of truth and invention, just like normal human beings.

Still, in the arena you draw your bull, and if he doesn't kill you… well. I've seen many a cowboy in a private moment behind the chutes wondering what the hell the bull-riding life is all about. I'm glad to be done with that phase of my trip.

Ike said thanks to me for my efforts just that one time, and as far as I know, not yet to John Woo, though they've crossed paths a couple of times. Eventually he will. And what are courtesies on the outside for anyway? A heartfelt wink or nod, conceding the first deal in a cribbage game, or calling a leaner a ringer in a horseshoe tournament, is worth a lot more.

For now, even though he's younger, he's older-brothering the hell out of me; getting kind of snappy about my habits. But until he's up and running, and able to get his own place, I'll put up with him. It's crowded, but he's family, you know.

If I were a true Mickey Spillane type, I probably wouldn't have spilled this story the way it happened, exhibited a little more craft, worked toward a surprising climax and a philosophical post-script. But even sober, I'm apt to spill the beans, even when I'm talking to myself. Still, being a detective—if I can call it that—is a career. I do plan to keep at it, after all I'm the only licensed peeping Tom and private rustler hustler in or around Fort Fletcher.

Ike says I live in the past, but unlike jailtime, something new is bound to happen. As I've explained to Pete more than once, things are developing as we wait. None of us will be able to outguess much of what's coming, even though we try.

I'll see. Ike's got me to thinking small. He says that way I won't miss something. And any true dog lover will tell you that you can never replace your favorite mutt, but Snickers is asleep at the foot of my bed. She'll give us puppies any day now.

About The Author

A few months back, I was asked to interview Warren Wendover. He was evasive, but finally opened up a little. It was clear that he planned to turn the tables. But I was still in charge of the interview and had the advantage of "the blue pencil."

Wendover: I gather my publisher sent you to do this interview.

Spence: Yes. And I appreciate you giving me an hour from your busy schedule.

Wendover: Not at all. You must be busy too.

Spence: So, starting at the beginning… where were you born?

Wendover: Well, where were you born?

Spence: In Sheridan, back in the good old days when my dad worked at the Burlington Northern tie treatment plant. My father was an itinerant chemist. Where he went, the family went. Laramie
eventually became the home base of my high school and college days.

Wendover: Sounds like as good a place as any.

Spence: Where did you grow up, and where did you go to school?

Wendover: My life probably isn't much different from yours. Everyone puts down roots somewhere… unless he doesn't.

Spence: How did you come by your writing skills?

Wendover: By imitating others. But you're generous to call them "skills."

Spence: Where do you live now?

Wendover: Buffalo, Wyoming. And just like you, I moved back to Wyoming in 1995. You gave me an honest job as dishwasher in the diner you opened on Main Street.

Spence: I gave you a job? That was you? You're kidding!

Wendover: I didn't last long, but everyone does what he's capable of, if he chooses to. (Pause while I refill our coffee cups)

Wendover (continues): I hear you've published a collection of poetry.

Spence: Yes. But this is about you. Let's go on with the interview.

Wendover: Sorry. As Groucho Marx sang, "I must be going."

Spence: Wait, a couple more questions— (Wendover stands, waves, and leaves.)